Penguin Books
Penguin Modern Stories 10

D0589872

Penguin Modern Stories 10

Edited by Judith Burnley

Penguin Books

Penguin Books Ltd, Harmondsworth,
Middlesex, England
Penguin Books Australia Ltd, Ringwood,
Victoria, Australia

First published by Penguin Books 1972

Made and printed in Great Britain by
C. Nicholls & Company Ltd
Set in Monotype Baskerville

Contents

Biographical Notes

All these stories are published
here for the first time in
this country.

Brian Glanville

La Brutta Verità

Milton Orchid and his wife lie side by side in bed, Gothic
and serene in sleep, their faces seamed, heavy featured,
middle-aged, tilted away from one another; his to the left,
hers to the right, as if in tacit, mutual rejection. Even in
sleep, Beth Orchid's full underlip turns downward in a wry,
defensive *moue* of scepticism. Her cheeks are round and high
boned, her nose, like his, a promontory. Her hair, so tightly
restrained by day, tugged back from the wide, pale forehead, imprisoned in a bun behind the head, flows free,
modulating; black hair, thickly streaked with grey.

Milton's hair is vanishing. Curly and dark, it has retreated from above the lined forehead, leaving sparse
pockets of resistance, making a provisional and uncertain
stand somewhere about the line of his large ears, ambushed
in the rear by a small surrender at the crown. His mouth, as
full as hers, hangs slightly open, his breath comes through it
like the slow hiss of steam from a pipe.

In a corner of the light, red-tiled room stands a bust he
has sculpted of his wife, in which she has become a Roman
matron, powerful and austere, scepticism turned to stoicism,
the nose, the lizard-lidded eyes, the mouth, all fractionally
and subtly changed to suggest the classical, rather than the
urban present.

Through the green wooden lattice of the *persiane* sunlight
comes, first playing on the woven red counterpane, then on
to Milton's face, like a beatification. His head turns to the
left, then to the right, trying to escape; his mouth closes, his

7

eyes open, then shut again, his right hand, from its white, cotton pyjama sleeve, stretches out to touch his wife, clutches her plump arm, broad, strong fingers, then, as if reassured, withdraws.

Slowly, though his eyes stay shut, his face is suffused by consciousness, a gathering tension. The mouth draws firm, the wrinkles on the brow converge like tributaries towards the nose, as if waking were pain.

Bad, bad, bad. Jesus, what's so *bad* about this morning? Let it come. It'll come, okay. It'll take shape, out of the cloud of *angst*, and then I'll deal with it. It can't be so terrible. Wait. Here it comes. Joe Kauffmann. But there's something else. Joe I can always deal with, if only just by not seeing him. Oh, God, yes; Vera. Jesus, Vera. I'm in love with her. I ... am ... in ... love ... with ... her. Which is ridiculous. Not true. Except that I told her. While I was giving her her private lesson. *Vera, I am in love with you.* It just burst out of me, I couldn't stop it, and the moment that it had, I wanted to apologise. It was simply too much for me, being so near her, to see her looking that way, so God damn young, so strong, so beautiful; her red hair against that wonderful white skin, but before I could apologize, she'd smiled at me.

She'd smiled at me like that before, I think maybe that's what triggered it, a kind of Garden of Eden smile, the most sensuous damn smile I've ever seen, as if she was saying, now, that this would be a secret between us; and then it was all I could do not to touch her, not to grab hold of her and kiss her, kiss those marvellous big breasts, squeeze those strong, white arms, and I moved away, it was the only thing to do. I was incoherent, I couldn't even look at her, but when I did, she was just working on the bust, like nothing had happened, just shaping at its nose, with her knife.

I was afraid she'd smile at me that way again, I was afraid she'd see I'd got this great erection, and what scared me even more, I guess, was that when she *did* see, it wouldn't worry her, she'd go on smiling that smile at me, again. I'm so ashamed of myself, now, I don't know how the hell I'll ever face her. I want to apologize, but I don't even know how to do *that*. Forty-eight, for Christ's sake, and she's seventeen. And with Beth, and everything I owe her. Everything I have.

I feel I want to explain to Beth, to tell her how it happened, so we can talk it over, put the whole thing into perspective, because I'm sure I know how she'd react to it, she'd laugh, she'd say, 'What *is* this, the twenty-three year itch? The male menopause?' Last night, I nearly did tell her, I said, 'Beth', then something stopped me. I don't know what the hell, maybe I was afraid I'd hurt her, though she'd never show it; or maybe it was just my sense of the ridiculous.

Milton?

Yeah?

How long have you been awake?

Around twenty minutes, I guess.

What's on your mind?

Nothing. There's nothing on my mind.

I've been lying here watching you. I wish you could see yourself. The Thinker.

Beth: there's nothing on my mind.

Okay, so there's nothing on your mind. Are you worried about Joe Kauffmann? We don't have to see him.

We never see him.

Do you want to see him?

Yes and no.

What does yes and no mean?

It means yes, I'd like to see him out of curiosity, no, I don't want to see him because sooner or later he'd get me mad at him.

So don't see him.

Sandro, the Persian cat, pushes the door open and comes with easy stealth into the room, his rich fur a luxuriant blue-grey, the colour of a cloud. Quite detached, each movement perfect in its sheer economy, he jumps, with equal ease, on to the counterpane where Beth lies, to be greeted by her cry of joy, 'Sandro!' Her narrow hand, the back white and glazed, moves caressingly through his fur. Her husband's joins it and their hands touch, move through the thick fur, then touch again.

You know, I think he may have worms.

He can't have worms. Just feel his coat. Just look at his eyes.

Nevertheless, I think he may have worms. There's a lassitude about him I don't like. He eats a lot, but he's lethargic.

He's pampered.

Who pampers him?

We both do. Hey, Sandro? *Sei un gatto viziato.*

Maybe I'll take him to the vet.

Sure. Did Joe say he'll call again?

He said he'd call this morning. I'll talk to him.

You don't have to.

Okay. I'll be missing such a lot, not having him tell me how big he's got.

He's doing pretty well.

Nine parts *chuzpah*, one part talent.

Chuzpah can be useful.

Did Michelangelo have *chuzpah*?

Michelangelo lived in a pre-industrial society where the artist still had a functional role. He didn't have to lose any time rationalizing what he was, he just *was*. And a patron wasn't just some ignorant rich jerk who'd been told he should invest in paintings; he was actually commissioning paintings. The Medici commissioning portraits. The Pope commissioning the Sistine Chapel.

When I get up every morning, I go across to the window, like I'm doing now, I push open the shutters, and I see what *they* saw, Michelangelo and Fra Angelico and Botticelli and Giotto and Leonardo. I see those same slopes, those same grey rows of olive trees, tumbling down to the city, those same tall clumps of cypresses, and *I* know who *I* am. I am part of a tradition.

In New York, what did I see? A lousy, ugly stoop, a decaying brownstone, garbage in the street, poor, ugly people. There is no such thing as urban poetry. Urban poetry is shit. It's when you can't live with squalor any more, so you romanticize it. You turn aesthetics upside down, what's ugly becomes beautiful. So you get pop art and welded sculpture, because you've given in. That's the real giving in, the real selling out. Staying in the middle of that crap and working there and thinking that you've beaten it, when all the time it's beaten you. Joe thinks he's beaten it. He's part of it.

I could stand by this window all day, just looking at the contours and the colours. At this hour, it's still very soft, like an underwater light. Later on, it gets harder, sharper.

The light on Vera's red hair.

Beth sends the cat off the bed with a lover's affectionate push. It lands four footed, impeccably balanced, stretches with voluptuous abandon, its eyes contracting to luminous, ecstatic points, then glides across the tiles and through the door.

Beth kicks the bedclothes off and, in the same movement, swings her solid, shapeless white legs to the floor. Plump and big breasted, she pads over it to join her husband at the window, throws an arm around his waist, pinches a fold of his stomach. After a transient hiatus, his arm rises, too, to go round her shoulders in a movement slow and enveloping.

This morning, you have your Torre dei Ghibellini girls. Figuratively, I hope.
Just History of Art, again.
And this afternoon, you go to Carrara.
That's right.
You know you haven't kissed me this morning?

Jesus, what is the *matter* with me? It just slipped out again, just like before: 'You want to come with me to Carrara?' Right at the end of the class, as I passed by her, at her desk. And she said, 'Okay', with that little smile of hers. No surprise, she never shows surprise, it must be a Serb thing, I guess; I've never known a kid her age so cool.

So here we are in my car, driving up the coast road, all those little *cinquecentos* buzzing around us like a swarm of crazy bees. She's wearing a white dress, sleeveless, bare arms, today her hair is piled up on the nape of her neck in that classical coiffe, a strand of it dangling down so it isn't too severe, and I feel happy, happy; guilty because I'm not guilty.

I'm telling her about things, Jesus, everything; I'm talking so fast and so much I'm like one of those lousy tape recordings that tourists plug in when they visit churches; you stick the ear-plugs in your ears and the voice goes on and on, telling you things you don't want to know. I've told her about the blasting techniques they use in the Carrara marble quarries, about the way they quarried it in Michelangelo's time, about the origins of the anarchist movement among the quarry workers and how you can find parallels in the Renaissance period, about the traditional methods of casting they've retained in parts of Tuscany, and God knows what else.

And she's listened with that smile, not saying a lot, I haven't given her much chance, though what she does say is always perceptive, it shows she's listened and she's understood, but the smile says she knows why I'm doing this, why I'm talking so much, so that in one way I'm longing for the drive to end, for us to get there, while in another, I'm wishing it would never stop.

I squeeze her arm, it's full but very firm, and she keeps right on smiling, she doesn't pull away or anything. It's one hell of a beautiful day, June weather, warm but not too hot. The coast road, once you hit Viareggio, is like shit, with all those bathing beaches and their lousy clapboard cabins, the fun fairs and those Gothic hotels the other side, but up above us inland are the Appenine Alps, which is where we'll be heading, it's clear and the shapes are beautiful, pink and grey shapes, the cloud lying soft on top of them. The marble looks like snow.

As we head inland and climb, it gets better and better, Vera keeps saying, '*Che bello*! *Che bellino*!' The mountains there above us, and down below us, the sea, which previously you only caught in glimpses between the bathing huts; today it's a very still, thick blue.

We turn a bend, and there are the quarries, like an Arctic waste. I never get tired of that first sight, that impact; it always amazes me, that blazing whiteness, like the world was beginning again.

When we get up there finally, we stand at the top of the quarry, looking down, which is something else I always like to do, to look down and think of all the marble that's been taken out of it, and taken out of all those hills, and what it's been used for, and by whom; the marble in the Medici Chapel, the marble in the Accademia, the marble in St Peter's. I am using this marble. I am working in this marble. They were going to show me the block they'd cut for me, and it was the *same* marble.

I had my arm round Vera's shoulders and I was telling her about all this; I was aware the men, the quarrymen, were looking at us, or rather at her, they were admiring her and envying me and they were giving one another those glances, wondering what it was I had going with her, when normally I'd bring Beth, and sensing this, I felt ashamed, I dropped my arm from her shoulders, but I was still happy.

Cevenini came up to us, the foreman, he's a tough little guy with heavy forearms, he said, 'I have the marble cut, if you want to see it', and I introduced him to Vera, 'La Signorina Musemic, one of my pupils.'

'Ah,' he said, 'one of your pupils', and I knew what the bastard was thinking; but how could I blame him?

The marble was beautiful; this big, rectangular block, dead white until you looked at it closely and you saw the whorls, the veins. I put my hand on it and felt it, virgin marble, cold and solid. 'Feel it,' I said to Vera, and she did. I looked at her; she could be a statue herself, so big and yet so elegant, every movement she makes so calm, so regal. She laid her cheek against the marble and she said, 'so lovely and cold', and looked up from the stone, smiling at me, sharing this with me, and suddenly, God knows why, Joe Kauffmann came into my mind, I felt a phoney, what was *I* going to do with all that beautiful marble? Carve another God damn lousy figure nobody would buy and no one would admire, except Beth. She'd admire it, okay, but that wasn't enough. It was not enough. It wasn't even enough for Vera to admire it, though God knows in that moment how much I wanted her to. I wanted the whole *world* to admire it, so she would admire *me*, and I felt so bad for wanting that, it was like physical pain.

And I was frightened of that block of marble, I was terrified of cutting into it, defiling it, because what it was now was beautiful, and unless I could improve on it, it was better that I left it alone. If there'd been no one else but Vera in the workshop – noisy as hell, with those saws whining into the marble – I'd have come right out with it, 'I'm no good, I'm no damn good', because the words were driving up in me, wanting to burst out of me, 'I'm no *good*', words I'd never dare say to Beth. And I'd have felt better for them, I knew that, they'd have purged me, I could maybe have begun again. The other words I want to say to her are, 'I love you.' And she'd smile.

I love you.
*Mil*ton!
I love you, and it's God damn ridiculous.
Why is it ridiculous?
I am thirty years older than you.
It makes no difference.
No *dif*ference? And I have been married for twenty-three years.
So long?
To a really wonderful woman, who has devoted her *life* to *my work*. To *enabling* me to work. You know in New York,

she went out to work for years as a stenographer, while I screwed around at home and sold nothing? Not one lousy thing.

But she did it of her own free choice.

Sure she did it of her own choice, that's exactly what's so marvellous about her. You never have to *ask* her for anything. And when she's done it, she doesn't want to be thanked. She doesn't want a thing.

Nothing at all?

Not one God damn *thing*.

And you are happy?

Of course we're happy. We've always been happy. That's what I don't understand. Why did I say this to you? Why do I feel about you like I do? What the hell are we doing in this car together?

We are driving to Florence. *Basta*!

Oh, Jesus, Vera, forget what I just said. No; don't forget it.

And the next thing I want to say, the next stupid, crazy thing, is, 'Let's take off together.' What scares me most is that I think she'd smile and say, 'Fine'.

I didn't call again, I just went right on up there, up to San Domenico, because I know exactly what she's doing, she's trying to keep me away from him. That's the way she sees herself, the job she thinks she does, protecting him from people, guarding his talent, when what she does is to shut in his talent, till in the end it shrivels up and dies. She wants that talent for herself, she'd *rather* it shrivelled up than got away from her, she's a very possessive woman and she's tied him up tight with all the things she's done for him, that she's made him *believe* she's done.

That's three times I've been here in these last four years, and three times I haven't got to see him. Every time a phoney excuse; he's sick, he's out of town, he's teaching. She can't forgive me because I've had success, but he's not like that, he'd be glad for me, if she'd allow it. And I acknowledge what he did for me, I'm grateful to him, I learned from him, but he should leave, now, he's hiding here, hiding behind her, hiding behind the tradition, which is his excuse for trying nothing new, for turning out the old, square, representational crap, graveyard crap.

And hiding in his job, teaching young chicks that look up to him because they don't know anything, impressing them with that History of Art shit and all the sentimental garbage about Florence. Florence is great. You come here and you learn and then you go away, and now and then you come back and you look again, not for too long; but if you stay there like Milton, Florence is death, Florence destroys you, and you stay there because you're scared to be alive.

I walked to San Domenico and it was a great walk, a grey and green walk, walls and trees, that pale grey and that very positive pale green, those steep lanes and the high walls and the foliage growing over them, and the sky that full Tuscan blue with thick white cotton clouds over Fiesole. I still dig it.

I knew what Milton would say to me. He'd take me out on to the balcony of that apartment of his, he'd swing his arm around, and he'd say, 'Where the hell else can you find a view like this?' and I would say, 'Nowhere else, but this view was here five hundred years ago. How much of your life do you trade for a view?'

Climbing the hill with a long, brisk, impatient stride, fractionally too long to be graceful, Joe Kauffmann turns, at last, beneath the scented abundance of leaves, into the gate of a villa, goes up its short path, at the sides of which grow pale hydrangeas. He has thick, straight black hair, large, dramatically dark eyes, a tanned skin, a thin, straight nose. He wears blue jeans and a maroon, short sleeved shirt, and emanates a restless, throbbing vitality.

The Persian cat lies basking in his path, and does not move. He stumbles and steps over it with a curse, reaches the door, around which runs a lattice of vine leaves, and rings the bell insistently, hard and long, till at last the door is opened by Milton.

Milton's face, startled at first, succumbs to an expression of delight. 'Well, Joe!' he says. 'Christ, Joe!' and reaches out, beaming on him like a father, to take him by the shoulders. 'You look so well! You look really strong and fit!'

'You're looking okay yourself,' says Joe, in a Brooklyn accent so pronounced that it hovers on the edge of parody.

'Wait till I call Beth!' says Milton. 'Hey, Beth, Joe's here!'

'*Joe!*' says Beth's voice.

She descends the stairs. 'Yes,' she says, 'it's Joe.'

'So who were you expecting?' asks Joe. 'Benvenuto Cellini?'

I went on up, and nothing had changed. He hadn't changed, she hadn't changed. The way they looked, the way they talked, the way they acted with one another; both of them with these Rembrandt faces, big, coarse, heavy features that can look very ugly or very remarkable. She's ugly, he could be remarkable, if his expression was different, if he believed more in himself, if he'd come out and take a chance. He says, 'I see you had a show.' He's basically very generous. She isn't. He said, 'I read about it in *Art News*. You had a show in New York,' and *she* says, 'Did you sell any?'

I say, 'I sold them all.' Then she says, she has to say, 'Milton's having a show. Did you hear about Milton's show?' and this embarrasses him, he tries to stop her, he says, 'Joe wouldn't want to hear about that.'

'Why not?' she says. 'Why wouldn't he want to hear about it? A show in the American Information Centre, American artists in Italy. Later on they'll maybe take it to Rome.'

I say, 'Great. What else are you doing, Milton? Still teaching all those chicks?'

'Still teaching,' she says, but very cautious. She looks at me very cautiously.

He says, 'I have to teach to live', and *she*, 'What's wrong with teaching?'

I said, 'With teaching chicks, nothing. I wish *I* was teaching chicks.'

'Milton just *teaches* them,' she said, and I looked at him, he looked very uneasy, which wasn't unlike him, and I wondered would she dig this, too, but she didn't seem to. 'Take him up to the studio, Milton,' she said, 'show him what you've been doing', like she was challenging me, I dare you not to say you like it, and he was sheepish about it, he said, 'Maybe later, let's have a drink, first.'

'You need fortifying?' she said. 'Okay, I'll fortify you', and she fixed us drinks, I had two Scotches on the rocks, and so did he. She said, 'Now, are you both ready to face it?' and we went up to his studio, an old attic, where nothing had changed, either.

He was working on the same things in the same way, all representational, all derivative, whether they were stone or bronze or clay, her looking at me as he showed me each piece with this kind of smile on her face, very nervous but daring me to say something bad, and while she was there I said nothing, I would not commit myself, just, 'Fine', and, 'Okay', and Milton I think dug this, because after a while he said, 'Do you want to eat with us, Joe?' I said, 'Sure, I'll eat with you', and she said, 'Okay, I'll go see what we have', and left us.

The moment she was out of the studio he said, 'How do you like them?' and I said, 'Like I always liked them.'

'What do you mean?' he said. 'Don't you see what I've been trying to do in these latest groups? The rhythm?'

Milton: you're doing what you've always done.

That is not so, Joe; why don't you look at it objectively?

I'm looking at it, and I see what I see. I see Renaissance sculpture.

You see the *influence* of Renaissance sculpture.

I see conventional forms, Milton. How can you be original through conventional forms?

Joe, they are not conventional forms. They're contemporary forms which happen to embody a tradition.

A tradition is something that you use. You go in and grab what you want from it then get out, otherwise that tradition is going to suffocate you.

Joe, I don't go telling you what I think is wrong with *your* art.

You did tell me. You told me many times. You had to tell me. Because if mine was right, then yours was wrong. So I left.

And you reckon now you've made it you've proved I was wrong?

I've proved that I was *not* wrong.

For God's sake, Joe, don't you think there can be room for both of us?

I had never heard him say anything like that. Not only the words, the tone in which he said them, like an exhausted man, a man who was about to give up, which was not what I'd wanted. I had wanted to convince him, but only after a long argument, maybe right through the night, in which he put his point of view and I put mine and in the end mine would win out, though I didn't really think this would happen.

But here he was, he seemed to have lost belief in himself, it was like some animal, stretching out its neck to be killed, and this I couldn't do to him. All I could find to say was, 'Come back to New York and see, come back to somewhere that's alive, come back into the present', then from below she called us, 'Do sculptors ever eat?'

Next day I said it, it came out of me the way I was afraid it would, 'Let's go away together', and she answered, 'When?' not even, 'Where?' which left me with my mouth open, because I hadn't thought beyond the question, I hadn't planned beyond it; I guess it was meant to solve everything on its own. I asked it or I didn't ask it, and if I asked it, it was like a magic formula; one way or the other, everything would automatically be taken care of. I'd maybe fantasized a little of *where*; the obvious, romantic places like Capri and Elba and Ischia. But 'when'? I didn't know when. Tomorrow, next week, today?

We were alone together in the school studio, I'd been giving her another lesson. My heart began to beat insanely, I couldn't speak, I could only look at her smiling at me, she seemed to be amused but it was a loving amusement, and all at once I bent forward and I kissed her on the lips, her hand went out, the one holding the knife, and she pulled me towards her, her tongue went into my mouth. When we broke loose I said, 'Tomorrow! Let's go tomorrow!' and she looked at me, a very thoughtful look, and nodded; a very grave nod.

I guess it was around six in the evening, I'd just turned off the Ponte Vecchio, and there on the left, at a table outside a little café what do I see? Milton and this great looking chick, holding hands and looking in each other's eyes, I couldn't believe it; but right while I was looking, he leaned forward and he kissed her, he was obviously mad about her, and from the expression on her face, a very tender expression, I could see she felt the same way – this seventeen or eighteen year old chick, a big girl, big and handsome, very majestic.

I was going to walk on by them, naturally, but at that moment he looked up and round and saw me, and the change in his face was just pathetic, so frightened and surprised. But now I couldn't walk on, and leaving him there to worry, so I said, 'Hi, Milton!' very casual. For a moment he looked at me like he was dazed, but *she* wasn't bothered at all, she was really very cool, then he said, 'Joe, this is Vera. Joe is also a sculptor', and he asked me would I like a coffee, so I stayed.

She asked me what kind of sculptor, and I told her, I told her how I had worked with Milton, then I said, 'What do *you* do?' and she told me she was a Yugoslav, she was studying in Florence.

Milton was very restless. When she said she had to go he said he'd go with her, but she smiled at him and shook her head, like she was saying that they couldn't risk it. She stood up, she was a big girl, she had a great body, and when she'd gone, I said to Milton, 'Congratulations, Milton, that is a fantastic girl', but he shook his head and looked depressed. I said, 'Milton, what's the matter with you? That kid is in love with you.'

He said, 'You think she is?'

I said, 'I know she is, I see the way she looks at you', and this encouraged him, he looked up at me, he said, 'I'm in love with her, too. We're meant to be going away together. I don't know what the hell to do.'

I said, 'You go with her, that's what to do, unless you're crazy.'

'And leave Beth?' he said, 'after all she's done for me?'

I said, 'What has she done for you? Maybe it's what you've done for *her*', but he shook his head, I couldn't convince him.

After twenty-three years, you just walk out on somebody?

But you told me already; you've decided to go.

Yeah, but leaving Beth.

Beth is a very strong woman. Beth would survive.

You think she would?

Milton, I know she would. But *you* would not survive. You are dying here, Milton. You have to face it. When do you get another chance?

You simplify things, Joe.

And you run away from them, Milton. You're making Beth your excuse, because you're scared.

Jesus, I ought to slug you, Joe.

You *know* what you ought to do, Milton.

On the drive back home, I suddenly thought of a possible way out. I was shaking and sweating, my hands were slipping on the wheel, I'd never been in such a state of mental confusion, one moment full of this terrible anxiety, the next so happy and excited it was like I was charged with electricity. I was dreading what I had to say to Beth, yet at the same time I couldn't wait to say it, I couldn't wait to go away with Vera, and then there were the things that I wanted to say to Vera, how beautiful she was, how much I loved her, and maybe more than anything how much I wanted to have a child by her, because ever since that moment, the moment she said, 'When?' this had been in my mind; that maybe after all these years I'd have a child.

As I drove through Florence I was aware that other cars were hooting at me, that I was driving very badly, taking risks, going fast, which was something that I never did in Florence, in those narrow streets. But somehow I got through them, round by the Duomo, up the Via degli Artisti, and finally, when I drove through the gate of the villa, Beth was there in the garden, she was cutting flowers, she was just so unaware of everything that I thought, how in hell can I tell her what I have to?

She straightened up and waved when she heard the car, she called, 'Hallo!' her arms were full of flowers. How could I hurt her and upset her? I could only think of what she'd done for me in all these years, and if she hadn't had kids, how could she help it? But as soon as I got out of the car she said, 'What is it? What's the matter, Milton?' and I immediately started to cry, I said, 'Beth, you must believe me, this is something I have to do for both of us.'

Do? What do you have to do?
Just for three months, Beth. Maybe for only a month.
Milton, will you explain yourself?
Look, Beth, I love you, but I'm in *love*.

She got so cold, then. 'Who are you in love with, Milton?'

With a girl in Torre Dei Ghibellini. A Yugoslav girl. Her name is Vera.

How old is she?

She's seventeen.

Milton, you're amusing me.

Look, Beth, look, darling, I do *not* want to hurt you.

In this, there's only one person who'd get hurt. Why can't you act your age?

Please, Beth, I want to avoid any bitterness between us.

So what am I supposed to say? Go off with your seventeen year old; I'll wait around until she's tired of you?

I'm not asking that.

Then what are you asking, Milton?

The right to fail. I just demand the right to fail.

'Okay,' she said, then, 'fail!' and went into the house and slammed the door.

I went walking after that, I walked on up to Fiesole. The night was beautiful; the scents in the lanes, the grasshopper noise, the air so very soft. I crossed the *piazza* at Fiesole and went on up the hill, stopping every now and then to look over the low wall down at Florence and the lights, thinking of what lay there and what I'd be leaving; Brunelleschi's dome, so rhythmic; Giotto's *campanile*, next to it, all the other towers and cupolas and perfect squares. The bridges I could make out by their lights, the Santa Trinità, the Ponte Vecchio, the Carraia, and way on down beyond them, the Cascine. I ached. How could I leave?

When I got back to the villa Beth had gone, and for a while I just went crazy. She'd done it once to me before, once in New York, after we'd quarrelled, and I remembered running blocks and blocks, like a maniac, till at last I came back to the apartment, and there she was.

She'd left me a note; one of her blue envelopes was lying just inside the door, the envelope had 'Milton' written on it, and the letter said, 'I'm sorry I've spent so much time trying to help you succeed when I should have been trying to help you fail. I think you can do that pretty well on your own.'

I looked upstairs, in the apartment; she'd taken one case, and from what I could see, a few dresses, some pairs of shoes, and things. The car was still standing outside, I'd had the keys in my pocket, so I guessed she'd called a taxi. Once again, I felt this confusion of emotions, worried and glad, anxious and relieved.

I went downstairs to our landlords, the Cudicini, these two old Florentines we didn't see too much of; they thought they may have heard a car draw up, but that was all. Then I called three or four of our friends to see had she gone around to them, but she hadn't; and several hotels, but she wasn't there, either. I poured myself a very strong whisky, I sat down and I tried to think it out, what the hell should I do? How could I take off without knowing where Beth was, whether she was okay? Because it was all planned; ten o'clock the next night at the Porta Romana, the foot of the *viale*, then we'd go South down the *autostrada* till we decided where we wanted to stay; no plans, nothing to tie us.

In the end I just went to bed, I was getting nowhere, and the curious thing was that I slept.

I woke up feeling very strange, not even anxious, just strange, till I realized why I felt so strange; I was alone in the bed. God knows how long it was since I'd been alone in a bed. I reached out and ran my hand across the sheet and it was cool and empty and this tremendous sensation of excitement welled up in my solar plexus. I jumped out of bed and had a look at the view. It moved me more than ever, now I knew I was leaving it and maybe never coming back to those gentle colours, that wonderful serenity.

Today I wasn't teaching at Vera's school, thank God, I was teaching at the Villa Tancredi, but just the same it was an ordeal. All day long I was thinking, is Beth home, will Vera come tonight? I was making ridiculous mistakes, confusing names; the girls must have thought I was drunk.

That evening, I drove back to the villa; I put my key in the lock, and I was trembling. I opened the door: no note. I called upstairs, 'Beth?' No answer. I went up, looked around and Beth wasn't there, but she'd been there. Another case was gone, a lot more clothes: and I felt a great relief. At least she was still okay.

I sat down then and wrote a letter to her, how much I

loved her, how much I hated hurting her, but this was something that I knew I had to do, maybe it would work and maybe it wouldn't, I was torn in two about it, and if it didn't work, I wouldn't blame her if she didn't have me back. I said I knew what she'd done for me, I'd be grateful as long as I lived, in fact part of the trouble was that now I felt maybe I'd exploited her and neither of us would admit it – this was what I'd meant about the right to fail – and if one day we could admit it, then maybe both of us would lead fuller lives.

Yet all the time I was writing this I felt a hypocrite, because I was so happy. I packed a case full of clothes, and I felt happy. I fried some eggs for myself, and I felt happy. At nine o'clock I got into the car, and happiness sprung up inside me like a fountain.

Then as I began driving down the hill into town I started feeling apprehensive; would she come? I hadn't spoken to her all that day; how could I be sure she hadn't changed her mind, that something hadn't come up, because I knew it was now or never, I was built up to it now, I was ready for it, but if she didn't come, the moment would have gone, it would be over. And yet I *was* sure, underneath the surface panic. That was one of the things about it, funnily enough, a thing she had with Beth: the integrity, the rock bottom honesty.

I drove across the Lungarno, over the Ponte alla Carraia; the gloves of light all down the Arno were like beads in a necklace, and high up ahead, among those black clumps of cypresses, there she was, Vera, getting ready to come down. I drove past the Palazzo Pitti, which to me was like certain women, sometimes beautiful and sometimes ugly, but tonight, maybe because of the mood I was in, it looked beautiful, grandiose there in the dark, with such a certainty about it, those giant stones; it overwhelmed you, and if it was *parvenu*, what the hell?

I went up the Via Roma, round the big gate, and there at the bottom of the hill I waited for her, sitting in the car, looking up the long *viale*, which looked beautiful, too, at

25

this hour, thick and black with trees, waiting, looking at my watch, wondering would she come. Quarter of ten, ten minutes of ten, then suddenly there she was, maybe two hundred yards away, wearing a white dress, sweeping out of the night like a galleon, very tall, very poised; carrying a case in her hand.

I was paralysed; overjoyed, yet at the same time, very frightened. Suddenly I thought of Beth, left on her own; how could I go through with this? If I did, I knew she'd lie in my heart like a stone. I still had time to reverse the car, I could turn right around, I could drive back, Beth would come back to me. Maybe she was waiting there now. My mind was a whirlpool, again; I want Beth, I want a child, I want to stay, I want to go. I closed my eyes and sat there, my hands on the wheel, hearing the footsteps now, getting louder, getting nearer.

Brian Glanville

Roman Summer

Meeting Jim at the airport was a mistake, I guess, it made him draw the wrong conclusions; but I did have a reason for it. Most everything else in Rome just happened, and I'd try to find reasons for it afterwards. Hanging on there just happened and meeting Sergio just happened and sleeping with him just happened and staying on in his apartment just happened. Nothing had been too real since we got on the boat in New York. The farther we got from the States and the nearer to Europe, the more unreal it was, until going ashore at Cherbourg was like stepping into a dream and arriving in Rome like a dream inside a dream, because Rome can't be real at any time, and Jim in Rome was unimaginable.

So I went to the airport like he'd asked me to in the cable, ARRIVE ROME 1800 HOURS THURSDAY MEET AIRPORT, because airports were kind of neutral territory. Meeting him on the Via Veneto or on the Spanish Steps would be just too traumatic.

But when I got to Fiumicino, that was Rome as well, in spite of all the metal and glass and the screaming of the jets. Maybe it was just the people, the way they looked and stood and talked and mooched around, treating it like a *piazza*, or maybe it was Rome itself, the aura of it, spilling over, so powerful that it touched everything around it.

One good thing about it though was that it relaxed me, I'd no apprehension. It was my dream, and if Jim walked into it, he couldn't touch me. There was this strange hum in the place, maybe from the air conditioning, the flight announcements seemed like they were coming in from outer space, and I guess I went off into a kind of coma; it was so easy in Rome, where everything was so tactile yet so transient, like a Cinerama movie.

And suddenly there he was, I saw him before he saw me, thank God. He was walking very quickly with his bag in his hand, looking so American it wasn't true, with his hair so short, almost crew-cut, wearing one of those olive coloured lightweight suits, looking around, looking for me. I sat and waited, at first I didn't call. I just sat watching the movie. For a moment I thought I'd let him walk right past me, then his head turned and he saw me, he said 'Karen', like an accusation. I said 'Jim?' and stood up, trying to wake, wondering how he'd be, whether he'd kiss me. He said, 'Karen' again, only friendlier, and kissed me on the mouth. I didn't kiss him back. He smelled of the usual shaving lotion, fresh and clean.

I said, 'Hi, Jim.' It sounded kind of dopey. He said 'Is that all: hi?' I said, 'Just for the moment.' He took me by the arm and said, 'Come on; I'm so goddam tired. I've booked into the Excelsior; is that near you?' I said, 'The Excelsior's near everything', and then, when he looked at me, 'Rome isn't big.'

We didn't wait for the coach, he called a taxi. In the back seat he took my hand; I let it lie there. He said, 'What's wrong, Karen?' and I said, 'You're not real, yet. Don't worry, though; you will be.'

He said, 'Who's real? This Italian?' But I didn't answer that, there was no answer; I just looked out of the window as the road went by, the crazy signs. Then he said, 'I want to see him tonight.' I knew the tone, I knew just the expression he'd have on his face; I didn't need to look. When I did, there it was, the one I used to call his Governor of Michigan look, like a recruiting poster, chin stuck out – he has a heavy chin – and blue eyes blazing into space. I felt a sigh rise out of me, I couldn't stop it, and I said, 'Oh, Jim!'

He said, 'What the hell do you think I came for?' I said, 'I don't know, Jim, I just don't know', and he said, 'For Christ's *sake*', tightening his grip on my hand, till I had to pull it away. He said, 'I came to bring you home.' I said, 'But I'm not *going* home. The ship doesn't sail for Naples till July 23.'

Then we were at it again like we'd so often been before, backwards and forwards, easier for him than it was for me, because he's always sure he's right and I always suspect I'm wrong. It's the businessman in him, the politician. You're going; I'm not. You are; I'm not. You're out of your mind; I'm not. I'll kill him, the lousy Wop; oh, don't be so childish. Then quiet the rest of the way till we got to Via Veneto, and the Excelsior.

At the desk, I said to him, 'I'll see you tomorrow, Jim', and it knocked the wind out of him, 'What do you mean? What the *hell* do you mean?' I said, 'I've got a dinner date. I'll see you tomorrow', and began to walk out of the hotel.

He came after me and grabbed my arm. I stopped, not resisting him. I said, 'Please, Jim', very calm, a little weary, always the best way to deal with him. Then words came sputtering out of him, questions; who are you meeting? *him*? when do I see you, for Christ's sake?

I shook him off and started walking again, he was saying, 'How the hell can you *do* it, go straight from me to *him*? I'm just off the goddam plane!' I said, 'I need time to think, Jim'. He said, 'Time to *think*! What do *I* need?' Then, at the railings, by the Via Veneto, when he saw it was useless, that I was in what he called one of my mule moods, 'What kind of rat would break up a ... relationship?' I knew he wanted to say marriage.

I said, 'He didn't know', and drifted off, not looking back, tense the first fifty yards or so, till I felt sure he wasn't coming after me. It was funny how quickly I forgot him, then, how he seemed to vanish when I turned the first corner, like he hadn't even arrived. I don't know whether this was Rome or me, maybe it was both of us, one acting on the other.

My college room mate, Julie Cohn, said to me soon after I'd met Sergio, 'You Mid-West girls are schizophrenic.' I'd asked, 'Why?' though I'd known what she meant.

She said, 'They shouldn't ever let you go East. Or once they do, they shouldn't let you back. It causes too damn much confusion.'

Julie's from New York and we might come from two different planets. We were kind of thrown together at Radcliffe when we arrived, and we've stayed together, through inertia, I guess – my passivity, her dependence – learning to tolerate each other. When she heard I was going to Europe, *she* wanted to go to Europe, and I hadn't the strength of mind to tell her go on your own. I want to lose myself, I don't want to spend my time there looking after you, picking your clothes off the floor, hunting for your jewellery.

I remember how she'd looked at me, meeting Sergio; on Via Veneto, he'd leaned across from the next cafe table, sitting with a man and a girl, and asked could he see my Paris *Herald Tribune*. I said, 'Sure', handing it over, and Julie gave me this indulgent smile, there-you-go-again. She was great at putting people down. Sergio caught the look, I think – he was quick and dipping, like a bird – but he took the newspaper and thanked me, then made a great production out of reading it, while Julie grinned at me and I just slightly raised my eyebrows; so what?

There was something Pan-ish about him, light and mischievous, with his long sandy hair, his long thin fingers, hollow cheeks. When he did start to talk to us, it was about the war in Vietnam, and that got Julie going right away; I think she'd like them to send her a draft card, just so she could burn it. He said he'd been out there for his magazine, he agreed with her basically, but it wasn't that simple. The other two watched; I guess they didn't speak English.

Next morning he called and asked me to dinner. I knew right then that I was going to sleep with him.

It must have been around a week later that he suddenly turned to me in bed and asked, 'You have someone in

America?' 'Yes,' I said. 'You are in love with him?' I said, 'I guess so.' 'And you are going to be married?' 'Yes.' Then he sighed, turned away again, and lay there on his back. He said, 'What is his name?' I said, 'Jim. He's in business school, in Michigan. I've known him a long time', and that was the last we ever mentioned it.

I was going to meet him now, at the Colony. I looked round once to see if Jim was following, but he wasn't. I knew if he saw Sergio he'd say, 'How could you?' and if Sergio saw Jim he'd say, 'How could you?' Jim so big and blond and solid, Sergio so mercurial; opposite poles, me drawn to both of them.

Sergio was throwing dice at the bar; as soon as I sat down he asked, 'What is the matter?' He's got antennae. I said, 'Jim's here.' It just leaped out of me, I hadn't meant to tell him; it was this strange thing again of being lived, not living.

He looked so startled that I almost laughed; it was something new to see him startled, his mouth open and his eyes popping; surprising people was *his* territory.

He said, 'But you are joking.' I said, 'No', and then he said, 'So you are mad. Quite mad.' I said, 'He doesn't even know who you are.' He said, 'But he has come to find out; otherwise why is he here?' I didn't answer, I just couldn't begin explaining things; what was real and what wasn't, what you expected and what you didn't. I should have warned him, I guess, but I didn't warn him because I didn't believe it, not till the moment Jim showed up in the airport, I couldn't visualize him in Rome.

Sergio said, 'You are good at keeping secrets. First that he exists, then that he comes here.' He sounded petulant. I'd sensed it in him before, this petulance, yet seeing it was new to me, like his being surprised.

He said, 'Come on!' and slid off his stool; graceful, as usual. He had his Giulietta Sprint around the block, and we roared off through the Piazza Barberini, Sergio driving like he always drove, as if it was a race; down the Corso, through the Piazza del Popolo and out on to the Via Flaminia. We didn't speak; I didn't want to; the Roman dusk was so beautiful I just wanted to enjoy it, the shapes and the smells and the colour and the feel. I wished we could just go on driving, in this marvellous limbo.

When he did speak, at first I didn't hear him, till he yelled at me, 'I ask you what you now intend to do?' I raised my hand with the palm up and shrugged, a gesture that I'd got from him, usually good for a laugh, but not tonight. He said, 'Nothing. That is how you solve everything, by inactivity', which wasn't fair – but again, how could I argue, in the circumstances?

He said, 'Placid women are the most dangerous, the ones who allow things to happen', then turned to look at me and said '*La Madonna Corrotta*'. I said, 'I'm not corrupt.' 'No, no,' he said, 'You're innocent, that's worse. You destroy people with your innocence.'

Oh, Sergio, I thought, please don't be so rhetorical, but I didn't say it, I gave him his little victory; Americans, corrupting Europeans with their innocence. At least it was a twist on Henry James.

I asked him, 'What are we doing, escaping?' We were passing Monte Mario; in the half light, it had lost that marvellous sweep of green; the trees were black, like spears against the sky. He was being ridiculous; I wanted to put my arms round him and hug him like a child. It was the way I'd so often felt about Jim, yet they were so different, fifteen years different, two Continents different, Jim taking everything like it was, Sergio accepting nothing.

Suddenly he turned off the Flaminia, then swung right again, heading back towards Rome. He said, 'I am not afraid of your young capitalist *buffone*; I just resent unnecessary disturbance.' I put my hand over his, on the steering wheel. I said, 'I'll see that he goes home.' He said, 'You should have seen that he did not come. Except perhaps you wanted him to come.'

That riled me, I told him, 'Don't be so damn *silly*!' and he went supercilious, shrugging, pitying me. I said, '*Look*', and went through what had happened, Betty Ryan in

American Express that morning, '*Hi* girls!' trailing us all over, checking in at our hotel, walking by the afternoon I came out of our room with Sergio, giving me that *I* won't tell look. Then going home to Detroit and calling Jim in Niles, I could imagine every word of it, 'Jim I'm so worried about Karen.'

I told him all this and he didn't answer. I said, 'Do you think I planned it?' but he just shrugged again. Then we were in Via Babuino, turning down the alley where he parked his car.

Getting out, he walked ahead of me, quite quickly, stooped, his hands in his pockets; far enough ahead to show he was still mad, not far enough to exclude me. For a moment I felt like letting him just go; I guess he sensed that, because he half looked round, then quickly back again, like he was ashamed of weakening. So I did what he wanted, I caught up with him and tried to soothe him.

He opened his front door, still without speaking to me, then half way up the stairs, in the dark, he turned and kissed me, roughly, almost aggressively, and, in the apartment, that was how he made love to me; like a revenge.

Afterwards he lay like he often did; on his back, insulated, hands behind his head, quite silent. His body was white and wiry, thick brown hair on his chest, an intellectual's body, mind over matter. Looking, I thought of Jim's body, thick and heavy, and I wondered how far bodies made people. A body like Jim's didn't leave room for doubt.

It was quite dark in the room. Sergio said at last, 'You will waste your life with him. He will imprison you.' I said, 'Perhaps.' He said, 'No perhaps. A man like that is frightened, *un povero di spirito*. He has no choice; or he brings you to his level, or he cannot survive.' I said, 'It's a lot more complicated.'

Next morning, after Sergio had gone to his magazine, I called Jim. He said, 'Where have you been, for God's sake? I've been calling your hotel all morning. Julie said she didn't know where you were.'

Brian Glanville

I said, 'She didn't. Jim: go home.' He said, 'Are you
crazy? I've just got here to bring *you* home.' I said, 'I've
told you, I'll come in my own time. Don't try and force me,
Jim.' And it seemed to me I'd been saying this for years, at
least the last seven years, through high school, through
college vacations, wishing he'd be more subtle, that he
wouldn't always meet me head on, making us go through
the same old thing; the rows, the sulks, the reconciliations.
I said, 'Go to Capri. Go to Sicily. Got to Florence. Take a
tour of Italy. Forget me just for the next three weeks.'

So he got angry, then *I* got angry, and in the end I said
I'd meet him next day for lunch in Doney's, a few blocks
from the Excelsior.

Then I called Julie, she said, 'Great to hear from you.' I
said, 'I'm sorry, I guess Jim's been bothering you.' She
said, 'No bother. Only three straight hours of him, yesterday night. The story of *his* life, the story of *your* life. I didn't
think they made them like that any more; look, no doubts.'
I said, 'Oh yes. They still do in Michigan.'

We met in the Caffe Greco, in Via Frattina, no one else
there that time in the morning, the perfect hour for a
conspiracy. The perfect spot with all that gloom, those
plum plush benches, those ancient posters on the walls.
Julie said, 'I kind of envy him. It must be great to believe.
He pumped me till my arm damn near came off; who was
Sergio? were you living with him? was he married? was it
serious? I told him Sergio was a journalist, that was all I
knew, I didn't even know his surname. I said, we're not
close friends Karen and I. Just room mates.'

I thanked her and she said, 'Well, isn't it the truth?'

We ordered cognacs, although it was so early, then we
talked about last May, when Jim came up for the prom, the
play he'd made for Doris Baker, how I'd sent him back the
ring, then how when I got home, we'd had an armistice.
But I'd still had to get away, over to Europe, and that had
been a battle too.

She said, 'Yeah, I mentioned Doris. After two hours or

34

so, it got to be enough, so I told him, I said, "You can be kind of provocative yourself." He said, "Julie, there's a difference." I said, "A difference between what a man does and what a woman does? A difference between what you do and what everybody else does?" But it didn't faze him; he kept right on being right.' I said, 'Oh, sure. He always does.' She said, 'And you still love him?' I said, 'This isn't him; not here. I don't think it's me. And anyway, you love people despite, don't you, not because?' She said, 'It may end up that way.'

She looked depressed; she was getting over something, she usually seemed to be getting over something, or else in the middle of something she'd obviously have to get over. Every boy she got involved with had to be some kind of a nut or a sadist. I had a feeling she was getting a kick out of all this, from the expression on her face, a half grin she sometimes wore, kind of wolfish. She said, 'Well, *I* think you're crazy if you marry him.' I said, 'You and everybody.' She said, 'Like Sergio?' I said, 'Yes.' She said, 'Well, that figures, but *I'm* objective about it. After last night, I'm beginning to get the picture; why he never came East to college, and all that jazz. Voted Most Likely to Succeed from grade school to graduation. Wow, does he hate the idea of reality!'

Next day, at Doney's, Jim handed me an envelope. He said, 'For your *Italian*', and I gave it right back to him, I said, 'I'm not giving it him, Jim.' He said, 'If he's a man, he'll meet me.' I said, 'He doesn't want to meet you.' He said, 'Then he knows I'm here. You've told him.' I said, 'Yes, I've told him', and he said, 'So he's running away from me. He's chicken. I'd like to give him this', and he held up his fist. I said, 'What would that prove?'

Sitting there, he looked handsome and arrogant. I knew that arrogance; it meant he felt uneasy, I'd seen it before when he was out of Michigan; in New York restaurants, at Radcliffe parties, it always embarrassed me for him.

He asked, 'Is he married?' I said, 'Separated', and he changed his tone, leaning over the table to me, taking my hand, looking into my eyes. 'Think of all we've built, Karen. Do you want to throw it all away?' I said, 'I'm not sure what we've built, Jim.' I really meant it; it wasn't said to hurt him. To hear him, you'd think we'd built St Peter's, but to me it often seemed more like some New York skyscraper, that you tore down when you thought of something better.

I don't think he really *was* hurt, but he acted like he was; 'How can you say that, Karen? After seven years.' I said, 'They've been strange years.' I felt very detached. Here, in the restaurant, with all the Roman chatter, and the sunshine coming through the plate glass windows, I was seeing him in isolation, like a behaviourist might, cataloguing tricks, analysing attitudes. I wanted to say, 'It's no use, Jim, your spell won't work in Europe, it just about makes it to the East Coast, and that's it.'

He said, 'You don't mean Doris *Ba*ker again, for God's sake?' I said, 'She was a symptom.' He said, 'Doris Baker was *nothing*! Look, Karen, we've been over this a hundred times.' I said, 'So why go over it again?' I meant it; it didn't bother me any more, there was only the shell of it.

I knew what was coming next, and it did. He said, 'When you have a real relationship, minor things fall into perspective.' I said, 'When a relationship's real, they don't happen. Please, Jim; it was you that brought it up.' I tried to change the subject, had he looked at anything; the Sistine Chapel, the Moses Statue, the catacombs. No, no, no, he said, he hadn't looked at anything, he didn't plan to, how could I expect him to? He hadn't come to Rome as a tourist. I said, 'But now you're here . . .'

He said, 'I'm here until I can take you back with me, and while I'm here, that's the only thing I can think about.' There was nothing to say.

Then he came in on another tack; my family. He'd been to see them, they were worried too, and that maddened me. I said, 'What have you been telling them?' and saw the pleasure in his face; at last he'd drawn me. He said, 'Oh, nothing specific, nothing to alarm them, obviously. Just that from things I'd heard, from things I read between the lines, I thought you needed me.'

A phrase of Julie's popped into my mind and nearly into my mouth, 'like a hole in the head', but I kept from saying it. He said, 'They're all well. Your brothers too.' Very solicitous. 'They all sent their love.' He'd always been a family-charmer.

I pushed my plate away, I couldn't eat. I said, 'Jim: this is the last time I'm going to see you in Rome', and he lost his cat with cream look. He said, 'I'll see you when I damn well *want* to see you', and I stood right up and walked out of the restaurant, it was no use staying. Again, he didn't follow me.

But you can't lose people in Rome, it's like a village, and as long as he was there it was going to be a strain; on Sergio and me, on Julie, too, which was even more unfair.

I apologized to her, I said, 'It must be such a drag for you. Maybe you ought to change your hotel.' She said, 'Oh, he'll stop coming round when the message gets through; that there's no sympathy; and that you've moved out.' I said, 'He may start tailing *you* – to get to me.' She said, 'Or bugging my room. Or tapping my phone. That's okay; it might be kind of fun. We'll use a code. I guess Jim might be better at it, though; he's got that C.I.A. look.'

I thought of sending him an ultimatum, if you don't leave Rome, that's the end of you and me, but it would probably just encourage him, a sign of desperation.

Sergio grumbled a lot. Whenever I was with him, he'd ask 'Is he still here?' I'd say, 'As far as I know.' Once I offered to leave his apartment, but he shook his head, very impatient. He hated being inconvenienced, but he hated the idea of being beaten even more. So there we were, living in this shadow; even when I was around Rome on my own it was there; was Jim behind me, would I see him round the next corner?

In fact he only jumped me once, after lunch in the Villa Borghese, in that heavy Roman heat that isn't like anything back home, the way it seems to hang and hum, like a

presence. Ambling down the paths, the green aisles, there
was hardly anyone around; just three soldiers on a bench,
calling after me; the kind of thing that bothers Julie, though
it soon stopped bothering me.

He came out suddenly from behind one of those bug-
eyed white busts, like from an ambush, smiling, glad to have
the upper hand. He said, 'Hi!' and I felt like hitting him. I
said, 'Haven't you gone home?' and he said in his most
provoking tone, 'Why should I? It's just getting interesting.
I'm zeroing in.' I said, 'You demean yourself, snooping
around.' He said, 'Look who's talking', but he changed to
his you-can't-hurt-*me* smile.

I walked away but he fell into step with me, saying he
knew I was living with Sergio, but if I'd go back with him,
we could forget about it. I stopped then and turned to
him, I said, 'Jim, what makes you think you've got this
power over me?' and his smile changed again, superior this
time, smiling down at me and saying, 'It isn't power, Karen,
it's just knowing *you*, knowing what'll happen.'

He ran his hand down my bare upper arm, moving close
against me! I said, 'Yes, you still attract me, Jim. I don't
deny it. But you don't belong here.' Then I walked away.
Behind me, he called, 'Neither do you.'

I'd get bulletins from Julie; what he'd told her, what he'd
asked her, though I had the idea that he was telling her
what he wanted me to know; he'd heard this about Sergio
and that about Sergio; he could find him now whenever he
liked, that he hadn't decided if he wanted to hit him, that
he knew he'd always love me.

After a week or so of this, I had a funny impression that
Julie was telling me what *she* wanted me to know; from looks
on her face, a kind of complicity, implying that she knew a
secret. I wondered had Jim been working on her, he's so
damn persuasive when he wants to be; she's sceptical, but
underneath, she's sentimental, very vulnerable. Then I'd
think no, I'm wrong, this whole cloak and dagger thing is
getting me.

Julie asked, 'Why don't you just get out of Rome? Go to

the sea, go to the lakes, to the mountains. Jim will get bored waiting for you', making me suspicious again; but I rejected it. Anyway, Sergio had said that he had to stay in Rome, and I wouldn't go alone; I'd feel like I'd been driven away. I think we both were waiting for the confrontation, though we never mentioned it; imagining it, preparing for it, so that when it did come, it was almost a release.

I'd thought of it maybe happening at Canova's, Jim striding across the Piazza del Popolo while we sat there – like a cowboy film, a melodrama – Sergio playing very cool, pretending not to notice him. Or in the Piazza di Spagna, round about twilight, the people flitting in the dusk like ghosts, Jim coming out of the dark and looming. Or maybe in one of those expensive restaurants, somewhere like Ulpia, near the Forum, Jim kicking up a scene, enjoying every moment of it; dead silence, everybody looking.

And in fact it just happened by coincidence, untidily; it was obvious Jim hadn't planned it from the surprise in his face. Walking down a street, the Via della Croce; over the cobbles, Sergio and I going down to Corso, Jim coming up toward the Via Babuino and *bang*! meeting. He still looked like an American vacationing, though he had a blue open necked shirt on, now, over a T-shirt, instead of his young executive's olive suit.

I could see him struggling, changing gear and mood, then he came up to Sergio with his hand out saying, 'Hi! I'm Jim Faulkner', like it was a challenge, Sergio looking at him, then at me, then back to Jim, before giving him his hand, just barely nodding. Jim's tone was loud and phoney and I ached for him, I ached for both of them, I wanted to fly off in a chariot, like Elijah. Jim said, 'I've been looking for you. Did Karen tell you?' Sergio nodded again, very tense and hostile; he didn't seem frightened, more wary, feeling his way. He put his hand on my arm and tried to take a step forward, but seeing this, Jim's smile went ugly and he didn't move. He said, 'We've got a lot to talk about.' Sergio said, 'We have nothing to talk about.' Jim said, 'Oh, yes, we have; a hell of a lot', still with this teeth

gritting smile, and all at once I felt sorry for him, he was
bigger and younger and stronger but none of it mattered;
not here in Rome, where he was a stranded fish and Sergio
was a fish in water, where I was with Sergio, not with him.
And feeling sorry, it was quite unbearable, I just had to
break up the whole horrible little tableau, and I grabbed
Jim by the arm, pulling him over to my right hand side,
moving down the street so Sergio came with me on my
left, saying 'We can't just *stand* here!' They were so surprised, they neither of them resisted.

There was a bar on our right, just over on the corner, and
I hustled them in there; we sat down at a little three-legged
metal table. The barman came out and asked us what we
wanted, and of course nobody wanted anything, he could
never have taken two more sullen orders than Jim's Coke
and Sergio's coffee, but at least the log jam was broken.

For a while, nobody said anything, Jim obviously screwing
himself up to speak, Sergio sneering at the Coke bottle, but
otherwise making like Jim wasn't there.

At last Jim looked up at Sergio and said, in this ridiculously formal way, 'You realize Miss Lennox is engaged to
me?' Sergio said, 'I realise nothing', and Jim said, 'Well,
I'm telling you', and there was silence again, while Jim
lined up the next one. I jumped in ahead of it, I said, 'Will
the two of you stop making me feel like Helen of Troy, or
something?' It was intolerable, both of them making these
silent demands on me, both of them waiting for me to
declare for them, and in Sergio I could sense something else,
his resentment at me for involving him. The moment
would come when I'd have to go off with one of them,
which would logically be Sergio, but I couldn't stand to see
how Jim would look. Yet if I just walked out and left them,
what would happen?

That was what I did, though, get up and leave, saying
goodbye to Jim and *ciao* to Sergio, not daring to look at
their faces, knowing both of them would feel betrayed; but
what else could I do?

Walking back up the Via della Croce, picturing them

still sitting there like waxworks, I wondered if Julie wasn't right, if I *should* leave Rome so Jim would go. It was good advice, even if she wanted me to go; and then I thought, Karen, you're getting *paranoid*.

Back at Sergio's apartment, I started packing; slowly, putting things in the case, taking them out again to re-arrange them, picking up my journal and reading it, look-ing at a guidebook. I still wasn't through when Sergio got back; I could tell his mood from the way he put his key in the lock, before he'd even shoved the front door open and slammed it. His face was all stiff with anger, almost planed; when he marched into the bedroom and he saw my case, he said, 'What are you doing? Where are you going?' and I guessed what he was thinking. I said, 'Away. Not with Jim. Just for a week or two. I don't know where.'

He rushed over and grabbed my wrist in those hard, thin fingers of his. He said, 'You are lying! I could tell in the bar. You have decided to go back with him!' I wrenched away and said, 'You're being as childish as he is. I sail home from Naples in three weeks, and not a day before.'

But it didn't stop him. I was getting to know his pattern by now; once he'd built up a head of steam like this, he had to blow it off before he became rational. So I sat on the bed and let him rant, listening to the rhythms not the words, just catching an occasional phrase, something about my being egoistic and irresponsible like all American women, something else about exposing him to imbecile peasants. When the words were coming slower, I said, 'I don't blame you for blaming me, Sergio.' He made a kind of disgusted noise, flung up his hands, then went over to the window, looking out. After a while he said, 'And American threats of violence. Always violence. I tell him, I will fight with swords like a gentleman, not with fists, like a ruffian. If you put your hands on me, I give you to the police.'

I laughed, and when he turned on me, I said, 'That must have surprised him.' He said, 'It astonished him.' I said, 'Jim with a sword . . .' and laughed again. Sergio I could imagine with a sword, it figured; nimble and darting, one with his character, winning out on skill, not strength.

He crossed the room, saying, 'So now you can unpack your things', pulling them out of the open cases, throwing them on the bed, while I pictured the two of them in there after I'd left, feeling sorry again for Jim in his pride, they were both so proud, wishing he hadn't done this to himself, created this caricature of himself, wishing I could show Sergio what else there was of him.

Sergio came up close to me, putting his hands on my arms; he said, 'After a week, we go to the sea.' When he made love to me it felt wrong, like he was celebrating a victory.

Next time I talked to Julie, she said, 'Sure, he told me. I get a daily news flash. I had *his* version though, he comes out of it better,' I said, 'Good, I'm glad he's living with it', yet I wasn't truly glad; Jim going to her for comfort, not to me, however unreasonable that was; how could he go to me?

I said, 'You're suntanned.' She said, 'Sure. We went to Ostia.' I said, 'We?' She said, 'Jim and me', and the message got through, the change in her, a kind of embarrassed satisfaction. She said, 'You can't go alone', meaning I'd deserted her. 'You lie in the sun, you don't have to listen.' I said, 'No, why should you?'

We were at Canova's, and I'd had enough, I said, 'I have to meet Sergio', and I left, crossing the Piazza del Popolo, so confused, so mad with both of them, with myself, with Sergio, that I didn't even look up at the view this time, the Pincio, looming like a brown and green wave.

I thought, what's she letting him use her for, the fool? and then, how cheap of him to use her, and then, how damn competitive of her, and then how competitive of *me*.

Walking, I told myself you're wrong, there's nothing in it, but I knew I was right; it didn't need what came, the grand revelation. I knew Jim, and I was getting to know Julie.

And Jim disappeared; if it wasn't for what I heard from Julie, I'd have thought he'd left Rome. Sergio was sticking his chest out; he figured that he'd scared him away.

The day before we were due to leave for Grossetto, for the coast, I went round to say goodbye to Julie; in siesta hour, when I knew she'd be there. I guess you could look back and say I chose the time unconsciously, but once you start playing that game, it doesn't have to end; so why didn't I call round in the middle of the night?

I went right up in the lift – officially, I was still sharing her room – and knocked on the door. No answer. I was going to go away, but I stopped a moment, listening, and I heard a rustle, like someone moving under a sheet. I knocked again, and this time, after a few seconds, Julie's voice said, 'Who is it?' I said, 'Karen.' She said, 'Karen; can you come back? I've been asleep. Can you come back in half an hour?' I said, 'Okay', and then I heard the cough, a man's cough, Jim's cough, I was sure of it, although it didn't have to be; sure that I was meant to hear.

Walking back to Via Babuino, I felt empty and depressed, though I knew it was irrational; even if it had been Jim. I'd had enough; of Jim, of Julie, even Sergio. I didn't want to go to Grossetto with this hanging over me. I had that Elijah feeling again, I wanted that chariot to rise into the sky and put me down in Niles, except that Niles meant Jim.

On the way home, I stopped off at a bar and had three cognacs, standing up; one, two, three. That got me by, and the next day was Grossetto, driving with Sergio up the *autostrada*, then a week in the sun, swimming, eating, making love, quite physical, forgetting.

Sergio changed by the sea, like most people do, shedding all his tension, wonderfully boyish, running round the beach, swimming, water ski-ing, having a ball. Watching him, I'd feel like a mother, taking her kid on holiday.

In a funny way, he was both older and younger than Jim. Perhaps it's an American thing that we're never quite young and never quite old; perhaps you never can grow old without once being truly young. Jim's ambitions stopped him being young, and when he was old, I could see him being like he was, right now.

Driving back to Rome, I wondered would he still be there, not bothered either way. Julie would have to be – or somewhere not too far, waiting for the boat. I had two different impulses, fighting each other, both irrational; one to forget them both, the second just to tell her what I thought about her. They cancelled out, and I did nothing; always so easy in Rome.

After a couple of days, it was Julie who called me, sounding very cautious and penitent; 'Karen?' I said, 'Yes?' in a weary kind of voice, which must have told her everything – she's quick – that I knew, that I'd forgiven her. She asked, 'Would you like to have dinner with me?' and I wasn't sure. Forgiving her was one thing, getting down to one of those confession-orgies was another. She said, 'I've found this place in Trastevere ...' Who with? I wondered, but I said, 'Okay'.

She was waiting for me when I got there, all melancholy under a jazzy fresco, wearing that pouty look I knew so well, her getting-over-it look.

I said, 'Hi. Has Jim gone?' She said, 'Sure; he took off for Florence, three days ago. He's still in love with you.' I said, 'He told you?' She said, 'It was obvious', and all at once I felt sorry for her and mad at Jim, the way he'd used her. She said, 'He'll make Governor of Michigan okay. He makes that unawareness work for him.'

Drinking made her more depressive still; we finished up on that bridge with all the headless statues, Julie sobbing, me with an arm around her, trying to comfort her, everybody's mother.

When I told Sergio about it later, he said '*E un vigliacco.*' I asked, 'What is that? A louse? Jim wouldn't think so.' 'No, no,' he said, 'this is the Puritan character. To do what you want, and afterwards to look for justification.' But Jim had none, he wasn't even a shadow now; there was only Julie, the shadow of a shadow. Otherwise Rome was like it was before, a fantasy; nothing but heat and beauty, and being with Sergio for these last two weeks. Nothing but living in the moment.

We made plans of course, like Sergio working in New York, me getting a job in Rome, but they were only gestures, fending off what we both knew; that we wouldn't meet again.

He drove me to Naples in the Giulietta, a crazy, hot drive that had me wondering if we'd make it and not really caring, though it wasn't fatalism, just the dream again, lasting until I got on the boat.

When he reached the quayside, the first face I saw was Julie's, looking at me from over the rail of the deck, big and sad. All around us kids were greeting each other, some were greeting me – 'Hi, Karen, how have you been?' swopping stories and places and boy friends, gawping at Sergio and me and whispering, giggling.

I looked at him and he was lost in it all, swamped by all us college girls; the quayside wasn't Naples, it was already America. I said, '*Ciao, Carissimo*,' and kissed him. He said, '*Ciao, Karen*,' very grave and gentle.

When I got to the deck, I waved to him; he waved once, very grave, still, then he turned and disappeared.

Julie joined me at the rail; she said, 'See Naples and want to die. I feel homesick for Rome already.' Then a Radcliffe girl we hardly knew came shouting, 'Hey, did you two get to Corsica? It's the greatest.' Julie turned and said, 'No', like Corsica was a disease, and she left us.

We were still standing there when they pulled up the gangway and weighed anchor, still there till way out in the bay, watching the purple shadows on the hills, and the water fanning out from the bow; moving out of the dream and into limbo, still there when Jim came around a corner of the deck and stood there, looking at us; here I am. Julie said, 'For God's *sake*!' like he was a ghost, but I didn't say anything, nor did Jim. We just kept looking at each other, he never looked at Julie, and I don't know which of us stepped forward first, maybe Jim, maybe me, but anyway there we were, in each other's arms, then kissing, and it all seemed planned, it all seemed kind of inevitable.

Brian Glanville

Three or Four
Cultures

I'd never seen anything like what went on at the airport,
when we landed. Talk about chaos. There were hundreds of
them, hundreds of Mexicans, little dark people, clapping us
and waving and wanting to touch us. All those strange,
brown faces, smiling at you. You had to fight your way
through to the buses; it was like running a gauntlet. When
we did get on to our bus, they stood and rapped at the
windows, all these teeth still flashing away. You'd have
thought we'd come from outer space. I said to Bobby
Wragg, our quarter-miler, who was sitting next to me,
'Phew! It's harder than running a race', but he said,
'Nothing's harder than running a race', which was the last
thing I wanted to hear, because I always tend to work myself up. I need someone to soothe me down, not worry me;
someone like Jack Drake, that's my coach at home, someone
to say, 'Forget it, Marion', or I'll brood. I'm a terrible
brooder.

It was miles and miles out to the Olympic Village, a very
dismal drive through ugly, tatty streets, terribly poor and
run down, till someone said, 'That's the Olympic Stadium',
and there it was, out on our right, this huge, white bowl. I
imagined it full of thousands and thousands of people and
thought, Oh, God, I've got to run there, and my stomach
flipped, I grabbed hold of Bobby's hand. He said, 'What's
wrong, Marion?' and I said, 'Just one of me turns, dear,
nothing serious.'

Then someone else said, 'Popocatapetl', and I looked out on the left. There were mountains, great, gaunt things, like nothing that I'd seen before, and I started wishing I was home, though I knew I'd be all right once I got there, to the Village, and I'd started training, because as soon as I'm on a track I'm okay, tracks are the same everywhere, if you see what I mean, even if one's cinders and another's Tartan.

And very soon we could see the Village, down on the right; huge, high, red, new blocks with coloured numbers painted on them. I didn't like the look of those much, either, to be honest, but at least we'd all be there together.

There were a lot of jokes among the boys about the Women's Village, how they'd have to use wire cutters to get in, or pole vault over the top. I told them, 'None of you can pole vault high enough, the only ones that get over will be the Germans and the Americans', and one of the other girls said, 'Very nice, too', which of course brought a great, big roar from them all, 'Well, hi, there, baby!', 'Vy you don't like us?' and that kind of thing.

The Village looked so big when we got into it, much bigger than than at the Empire Games. When we got to our block in the women's part, I had to go up three flights of stairs to my room; I was sharing with Mary Gregg and Joan Paulton, four hundred metres and javelin, and the first thing we did was try and make it cosy, sticking up all the photographs and pennants and things we could. Mary had a great, big picture of the Beatles and I put my bears all over the place, Rufus the big, pink one and Dylan, the green one, and the blue one, Ringo; Joan had a gramophone and put on a Stones record, till in the end it was quite like home, even if the cupboard space was terrible, just one measly little wardrobe and a chest of drawers between the lot of us, so we had to leave half our things in the cases.

Of course, what was driving everyone up the wall was the altitude business, would it affect us, would we acclimatize in time? My race, the two hundred metres, didn't carry an oxygen debt, thank goodness, but you still had it on your mind, you couldn't help it, and when we came into our room Mary collapsed on the bed, she was always larking about, shouting, 'Oxygen, oxygen! Bring me an oxygen mask! I can't breathe, doctor, I can't breathe!'

Joan said, 'Here's your oxygen mask!' and shoved a pillow over her face, but it wasn't really any joke, and when we got outside, Joan said, 'Hey, we'd better hold on to one another, in case anybody folds up', and we walked along very, very slowly, arm in arm, anyone looking at us must have thought we were drunk, till after about fifty yards Joan said, 'I think it's all right', she was in the middle, and let go of us both very slowly.

But in fact you found that even if you just walked quickly there was this tightening in the chest, this heavy feeling after in the legs. It was ghastly.

In the city, the white dove on its black background flew everywhere: Todo es Posible en la Paz. *There was an air of vibrant hiatus, a lull between battles.*

A week before, the tanks had been out in the Zocalo. In a side street, eight single decker buses stood, like wounded elephants, charred and gutted. Their survivors, yellow, dirty, made their laboured way down the Paseo de La Reforma, ships in a beleaguered convoy, their front windows pocked and starred by bullets, their sides black with slogans: DIAZ ORDAZ ASESINO, GRANADEROS ANIMALES. *Young mestizos swarmed on their steps, clung to their rails, poised like statuary.*

The white buildings, the green expanses, of the University stood empty, but for the occupying soldiers; small, bored, enigmatic Indians. The students remained on strike.

Outside the schools which they'd invaded and desolated lounged the riot police, the Granaderos, squat, swarthy men, jowled under blue helmets, hung with guns and gas pistols and respirators, their plump faces set in a thin, derisory smile.

Though the sun shone, a low, grey haze pressed on the city. Fumes of exhaust smoke hung, insoluble, in the mountain air.

We didn't train for the first couple of days, just lounged around the Village, which was nice, really; there was a smashing swimming pool and the sun shone and we got brown. The breathing was all right so long as you didn't hurry and the food in our restaurant was quite good. Of course we couldn't drink the water, which was rather a drag, and we took our two little pills every day. We made a big joke of it in our room. Whenever Lucy Grainger came round, our team manager, Mary would yell, 'Lucy, Marion hasn't taken her pills today!' and Lucy would say, 'Well, we'll just have to administer them forcibly', and I'd say, 'No, anything but that, I'll take them, I'll take them, I'll even swallow them without water!' Though we did hear about a couple of Americans who'd drunk the tap water and they were absolutely shattered.

Sometimes I went along to the track, which had a really gorgeous surface, Tartan. I'd sit there on the steep, green bank and watch the people training I'd be running against, sometimes clocking them, especially Martine Lechantre, the Belgian girl I'd beaten in the European Games. She had a very good action, with those long legs of hers, but I knew I started better, I was stronger. She'd run 23.1 in the Little Olympic Games, the year before, where my best this year, in fact my best ever, was the 23.2 I'd run at Crystal Palace, but I didn't take that too seriously, because everyone knows that in Mexico times are so much faster, sometimes in the sprints by as much as a couple of seconds.

When I did start training, I missed Jack dreadfully. The official coaches were all right, they tried to help, but it's never the same, you need your own coach, and Jack just couldn't afford to come, he was miserable, though he wrote to me every day, which was a tremendous help; how I should plan each day's training, when I should rest, what times I should be aiming for.

There was the Russian girl, Beskova, too. She was very strong, more like a man, I sometimes wondered how she'd passed the sex test, but I'd beaten her in the European Games, too, and I knew I could do it again, I knew I had a much faster finish.

It was nice, in a way, to be able to watch them without

their being able to watch you. I'd lie back there in the sun-shine on the bank and sometimes wave to them and wish it could go on like this; only, of course, it couldn't.

When I did begin to train at last, it was hard for the first few days, not so much when you were actually running as afterwards, when you had to recover, panting away for air that wouldn't come, frightened it would *never* come. I felt so sorry for Laura Bates, in the 800 metres, she had the room upstairs. After the first day's training she was practically flaked out, she lay on her bed and said, 'I'm dying, I know I'm going to die. I'd leave you my spikes, Marion, if you hadn't got such big feet.'

That first week, I did hardly any stamina work; Jack had told me not to. A few hundreds, well spaced out, a few two hundreds, but not the real interval thing, because it just took too long to recover.

There was quite a good atmosphere in the British team, everybody very friendly, but I think it was harder for those of us who were expected to win medals, because we were so few, only three or four; the others could relax more be-cause they hadn't got the same pressure on them. If *we* did well, it was only expected of us; if they did badly, nobody would blame them.

I got photographed a lot, and once you went outside the Olympic Village, there were all the Mexicans, again, sur-rounding you, trying to sell you things, asking for your autograph, touching you. We all bought masses of stuff, Mary and Joan and I; straw sombreros and bead handbags and paintings on bark and Indian jewellery and strewed them all over our room till it looked like a junk shop.

Just nearby the Village we'd sometimes pass a terrible little shanty town, tiny little one storey brick houses more like pig sties, some of them painted very jazzy colours, which in a way made them look worse. It seemed funny, somehow; us living there in these great, tall blocks, com-plaining about the cupboard space, and practically next door, these shacks. One or two of the boys said they thought it was a scandal, but I must confess I didn't think about it much, I'd come here for one thing, to win my event, and if I didn't do that, I'd have let everybody down.

That was what was in the air at the Village, under all the jokes and the chatter, that was what gave it its atmosphere; everybody wanting to win, whether they were black or white or brown or yellow, runners or jumpers or rowers or swimmers. There were Indians in turbans and Africans in coloured robes and Japanese in spectacles and they were all there just for this one thing; to win. No wonder it was so difficult to sleep at night. Then I met Antonio.

It was one morning in the athletes' lounge, a big room they had with chairs and newspapers and sofas, rather stuffy, and down below a basement where you could get coffee and Coca Cola and things for nothing – if you wanted them.

He was enormous but terribly handsome, like a gladiator; not huge like the shot putters and people, who've been on the anabolic steroids and blow up like balloons, but just terribly muscular and strong, great big arms and an immense neck, and this very clearcut, handsome face with blond curly hair, really fabulous. I think he must have felt me staring at him, because suddenly he turned towards me and stared back, and of course I looked away at once, shy little thing. That was one thing I'd promised myself before I came, there wasn't going to be anything like that. I'd come to win my races, and until I had, nothing was going to distract me or interfere with me, absolutely nothing and no one.

In a minute or two he strolled over to where I was sitting, there was a newspaper rack just by me, and I was wondering, will he speak to me, will he turn and talk to me, my heart was thumping away even though I knew it was silly, I knew I mustn't get myself involved.

Then he did turn, he did talk to me, he turned and smiled, he said, 'Do you understand English?' I said, 'Yes, I do, I *am* English, actually', it all came tripping out, I must have sounded quite gormless; I could hear the two girls beside me on the sofa, Mary and a long jumper, Beryl, sniggering away.

He said, 'Then tell me please what this means', and he
held out the local rag they have there in English, the *Daily
News*. There was a picture of some gigantic Russian girl
lifting a barbell with a little Mexican watching her with his
mouth open, and some funny caption underneath. I tried
to explain it to him and he nodded, there was something
very calm about him.

He said, 'You are a runner?' I said, 'Yes, I'm a runner
and she's a runner and she's a long jumper. What are you?
Don't tell me; let me guess. You're a discus thrower.'

'No,' he said, 'I am a wrestler.'

Mary said, 'Well, you're big enough.'

He said, 'I have to be big, I am heavyweight', then he
introduced himself, all terribly elegant, he bowed, he said
he was Antonio something or other. I asked, 'Are you
Italian?' He said, 'Uruguayan', and I said, 'Where's
that?' and Mary said, 'South America, you fool.'

His English wasn't all that good, he couldn't always
understand us, but we got along; we went downstairs into
the basement and we all had Coca Cola, he said, 'I hate it,
but I drink it.'

When the other girls left to go swimming I said I'd join
them later. They said, 'All right, *we* understand', very
sarcastic, then Antonio and I were left alone.

It was one of those click-click things that sometimes happen to me and I wish they didn't, especially at times like
these. He didn't say much, just stood smiling down at me.
I wanted to go but I couldn't, I seemed to be hypnotized,
I think if he'd said, right there and then, 'Let's go to bed',
I would have gone. There was so much in his face, such
strength and such a lot of understanding. In the end we just
went out for a stroll across the Village and ended up sitting
on the bank above the track, holding hands. I don't know
who took whose, whether I took his or he took mine; it just
happened. I could see two of the British men's team in their
red tracksuits looking at us over the parapet, but I didn't
care. I never do at times like this. Perhaps it would be better
if I did.

On Wednesday evening in the Zocalo, a group of student leaders from the Consejo de Huelga, the Strike Council, addressed a meeting. With the serene bulk of its colonial palaces, the Zocalo was a haven from the city's cheap modernity; its boulevards of lethal traffic, its synthetic Americana of coffee shops, skyscrapers, twilit bars.

The crowd grew quickly, filling the square, boiling beneath the students and their microphones, its mood intransigent, its cheers directed not merely to the students in front but at the Presidential Palace, behind. When the tanks rolled into the square, guns turning, probing, like the blind tentacles of octopi, the crowd gave way before them sullenly at first, till the police moved in behind the tanks and the square turned into a maelstrom of flailing sticks, fleeing men, falling bodies. Guns flamed now and then in the dusk, a student roared defiantly into his microphone till suddenly his voice stopped. Gradually the square was cleared, till at last there remained only the tanks, the police, the scattered bodies.

The place he took me to that afternoon was the Museum of Anthropology. Fabulous. I've never really gone for museums, I'd probably never have seen this one if it wasn't for Antonio wanting to go, but when we got there it was fascinating, very modern and not like a museum at all. They'd really tried to make everything interesting instead of just sticking it in glass cases so you could take it or leave it.

Outside they'd got this huge, carved stone Aztec pillar with water cascading all around it, marvellous, and inside the rooms were all lit up like an aquarium, full of these frightening Inca and Aztec masks, animal heads, and creepy descriptions of human sacrifices. I said, 'I'm glad they're not living here now.' Antonio said, 'In some ways it is worse', but I didn't know what he meant, then.

There were quite a few other couples there from the Village, athletes and their girl friends, it seemed quite a popular place. In fact some of them were so busy snogging they didn't seem to be paying much attention to the museum, especially one Italian couple who were walking through the rooms very slowly, arms around each other, looking into one another's eyes, till you wondered they didn't bump into something. Antonio looked at them and laughed, then, as we came into the next room and there was no one in it, he kissed me.

It wasn't the first time, but it was still all new and marvellous. I could feel him hard up against me. He was so strong I couldn't have pushed him away if I wanted to, and the trouble was I didn't want to. I was in a panic; part of me kept wanting to fight him off, the other part didn't, especially when I was with him like this, and being me, I knew which part would win. The thing was, could I hold out long enough, could I keep him at bay till after the final? At this rate I knew I wouldn't. I wouldn't even get through the heats. Lying awake in the night, away from him, I'd think about it and I'd come out in a cold sweat. I'd told him, 'Look, Antonio, I think you're smashing, you're super, but I've come out here to *run*, can't you understand that?'

He'd said, 'Yes, but you cannot run all the time!' It was hopeless. I knew so many girls who'd messed up their chances in important races, Empire Games and European Games and so on, just through this sort of thing, and I jolly well wasn't going to be one of them. I owed too much to too many people, and I owed it to myself.

As we came into another room, there was a boy and a girl in Mexican Olympic blazers that Antonio said hallo to. He introduced me, then they talked in Spanish, all very serious, though of course I didn't understand a word, till Antonio put one arm round the boy's shoulder, the other one round mine, and the four of us went downstairs, to where they had a cafeteria. We sat down at a table with our coffee, and the three of them carried on their conversation, very low, looking round now and then as though they were afraid of being heard.

I got a bit restless, to be honest, not being able to follow any of it, though now and then Antonio would wink at me and pat my hand and say, 'Sorry, sorry.' We must have been there half-an-hour, with me getting more and more fidgety, which I do anyway when I'm building up to an important race. I can't keep still, I have to keep doing something, moving around, like a racehorse in the paddock. Then at long, long last the two Mexicans got up to go.

I asked Antonio, 'Whatever was all that about?' He said 'His brother is in prison.' I said, 'In *prison*? What's he done?' He said, 'He is a student leader.' I said, 'I don't understand', and I didn't. 'Why should they put him in gaol just because he's a student leader?'

Of course I'd read about what happened in Paris, the demonstrations, fighting with the police and all the rest, there'd been a lot about it on the telly, but I'd no idea the same sort of thing was going on here. As far as I was concerned you came to these countries, you ran and you went away, you'd got enough on your mind with your own races, you just *had* to shut everything else out.

Antonio said, 'Many students have been killed here, many others are in prison. Have you no student movement in England?'

I thought a bit and remembered some strike or other at the London School of Economics, students sitting down in the entrance. I said, 'I suppose we have, I don't really take much interest', and he smiled and shook his head. I told him, 'I'm one of your ignorant athletes, I'm afraid.'

He tried to explain to me, then; what was happening in Uruguay, what was happening in Mexico, how the university students were on strike and the Army had occupied the university, how it had blown down the door of a school with a bazooka, the sort of thing you see in the cinema. What with his English and me being so thick about that sort of thing, I didn't really follow a lot of it, and besides, when he was talking I loved to look at him, his expressions, especially when he was so serious; very stern, and now and then this fabulous smile. It distracted me.

That night when we got back I went out on the track and I ran six hundreds, eight two hundreds and a couple of quarters. My recovery rate was miles quicker, now.

On Friday evening in the Plaza de las Tres Culturas, a 'mitin' was held by the Student Strike Council.

The square was colossal and amorphous, an immense, jarring co-existence of different epochs, irreconcilable moments in time; a paradigm of Mexico itself. First, the excavations, the Aztec remains, rising like stone whales out of a sea of grass. By them, the colonial church, built from the same stone, at once rugged and exotic, intransigent and bizarre, as if its builders, inexorable conquerors, had been touched despite themselves by what was in the air, by the arcane mysteries of the place. And all around the square, the shiny functionalism of the new, the yellow, corrugated cliffs of worker's flats, born out of the anonymous present.

In one corner of the square, Granaderos lounged, with their Saurian smiles, outside a school which had been closed. In its dusty centre, by a wall, stood Polytechnic students, small and poor, full of a throbbing intensity of grievance.

From behind the square there could be heard the thump, thump, thump, of a relentless drum, where Indians were dancing in a little market place. They danced tirelessly, without joy, bidden by the drum, the drum itself beaten by a fat, middle-aged woman, her face fixed in a showman's smile. A whole family danced; the man like a fine circus animal, marvellously muscled, his brown, thick legs descending with a stamp, as though on some hated face. He wore only a loincloth and a high feathered head dress; the expression of his high cheeked, narrow eyed face was perfectly impenetrable. He danced as a slave might dance who had translated resignation into something positive and challenging, making the best of a bitter predicament.

His wife, by contrast, danced without the same defiance, a slight, worn woman in a black shawl, each step a small victory over weariness, while their children, a boy and a girl, danced rhythmically, though they, too, had their father's impassivity without his challenge. Thump, thump, thump, went the drum as if worshippers were being called to attend a sacrifice, when they were being called only to buy.

Into the great square, an hour before the meeting was due, rivulets of people trickled. Imperceptibly, in small agglomerations, the crowd grew big, gathering in front of the yellow apartment block beside the school, from one of whose balconies the students would speak. The crowd, as it increased, was very quiet, expectant, but *without the aura of fear. By the time the student leaders filed on to their balcony and set up their microphones, it must have numbered four or five thousand, dense but not congested, mild but determined, easy in applause. Amongst it, paler, alien faces, foreign journalists and cameramen moved, scribbling and focusing and clicking. Students moved among it, too, spreading blurred, mimeographed sheets of paper like confetti.*

When the leaders began to speak, it was with raw inexpertise, hollering at the microphones as though they, too, had to be convinced, their words coming in distorted thunderclaps, the crowd responding fervently to each peroration: 'Justice ... the corruption of the Government ... the brutality of the police ... we shall go out among the peasants.'

Suddenly it began to rain, not gradually but instantly, great gouts of water falling on the crowd like a punishment, the crowd accepting it and bearing it, shifting a little as in gentle protest, putting up coat collars here, newspapers there, but still unscattered.

Honestly, I'm going round the twist. What with everything that's happening, I'll be surprised if I even qualify for the semi-finals.

One thing I am *not* going to do is give way to Antonio; I've told him a dozen times but he still won't believe me. That's the trouble with your actual Latin male, he'll never take no for an answer, not even a qualified no, and it's very hard, because I want to as much as he does, or rather I would do if it wasn't for these being the most important three weeks in my life. But it's no use telling him that, either; he just laughs. I said, 'How can you expect a wrestler to understand?'

When I've won, if I win, it would be lovely, but until I do, I need everything, every atom of strength, every ounce of concentration. Sometimes I watch those Russian girls and I really envy them, *they* don't have these awful distractions. I watch them thumping their way round the track and I know they're giving it everything, because it's all they've got to give it to, so unless I give it everything too, what chance have I got?

I've done a 23·4 and a 23·5, but I know Lechantre has done a 23·3, and the Polish girl, Juskowiaka, is meant to have done a 23·1. Lechantre's going really well, it scares me to watch her, but then she's always been better in training than in competition; I've always been better in competition than in training. I need all that, the crowd and the pressure. I flutter like a leaf, but it still brings something out of me.

Antonio came and watched me train now and then, he even timed me. But I asked him in the end not to come, it distracted me, not just because I have this thing about him but because of his attitude, his not taking my running seriously. I watched him wrestle once or twice, in the gym, heaving and hauling away; I told him one day it was like watching whales in labour. But he's incredibly strong.

On Monday morning, the mothers and sisters of imprisoned students began a silent march of protest through the city, from the Memorial of the Mother.

The memorial stood in a small square, north of the Reforma, abstract, squat and almost wilfully ugly. Beneath it was carved an inscription: TO HER WHO LOVED YOU BEFORE YOU WERE BORN.

The women gathered quietly, quite cheerfully. Though some, a little unsurely, carried placards and banners, they had an air of hope rather than despair, of cheerful unity in positive action. Most were middle-aged, a few were young; most poor, dressed in the self-negating black of the Latin woman who has resigned herself wholly to motherhood.

The procession took shape slowly, like molecules coming gradually together. While the women moved, unhurriedly and amiably, into file, a motor coach full of students drew up beside them in the square, and they broke into a smiling, spontaneous patter of clapping, the students smiling back at them through their windows, happy to be heroes.

As the students climbed down from their coach into the square, a dark man spoke sternly to them through a microphone. 'This is a silent demonstration of protest. A peaceful demonstration. You may

*walk beside it, but you may not take part in it. You must not inter-
fere with it in any way.'*

*When at last the procession, and its vanguard of banners, were
ready, the column began slowly to move out of the square, a sluggish
stream, a snake uncoiling, gathering pace, momentum as it did, filing
down into the Reforma among the traffic, the yellow buses and the
green collectivos, the honking cacophony of cars. Of these, the
women took no heed, as if, once started, there was nothing to stop
their gently irresistible progress, or their cause itself. The students
marched peacefully beside them, policemen looked on complaisantly.
The women did not speak or sing.*

I'm afraid I've let it happen. Between me and Antonio.
All I can say in excuse is that yesterday afternoon I ran a
23·5, in fact I think that had a lot to do with it, it was the
mood I was in; not only feeling chuffed, but thinking, it
hasn't done me any harm, being distracted; if anything, it
seems to have done me good.

I'd arranged to meet him that evening by the Post Office,
after I'd trained, and when I did I was absolutely full of it, I
said, '23·5, I did 23·5', but he just gave me a glassy sort of
smile. I said, '23·5, on my own, with nobody pacing me;
the winning time in Tokyo was only 23!' He said, 'You are
wonderful', and he kissed me, right there, bang in the
middle of the Olympic Village, and suddenly, pressed up
against him, I wanted to make love, I didn't care any more,
and he felt it, I could tell, because he didn't say anything,
just put his arm round me and we walked across the Village
to his block, the Uruguayan one, and upstairs to his room,
without anybody stopping us. He locked the door, and we
made love; it felt marvellous, having him inside me at last. I
felt full of life, full of power, and I knew that I was going to
win; the heats, the semi-final, the Final, all of them.

When he asked me next day would I go to a meeting
with him that Wednesday, a students' meeting, I said yes,
I'd have said yes to anything. That afternoon, I went out
again and ran a 23·4.

A march had been planned, to the occupied school at San Tomas; soldiers and their trucks, their tanks, girdled the Plaza de las Tres Culturas. When the first of the student leaders to speak announced that the march had been abandoned, the crowd gave up an instant, responding sigh; of surprise, relief, acceptance, disappointment. It was dense again, numbering perhaps five thousand; tranquil, as it had been five days before. The student leader assailed it through the microphone; democracy ... equality ... solidarity with the Olympic Games. As he spoke, the sun fled from the sky and night came very quickly, the square lit patchily now from the apartment windows, and a scattering of lamps. It was quite dark when the two helicopters came throbbing and droning above it, like giant insects in a mating ritual.

It sounded rather exciting when Antonio told me about it, going up on this balcony with all the student leaders, while they made their speeches. We were going with this Mexican friend of his, the one whose brother was in gaol, Manuel.

We got a taxi out to this vast, great square, swarming with people, where they took us into a block of flats, up in the lift, through one of the apartments, then out on to a balcony, where we looked down at all these people. There was a church down on the left and what looked like some ruins, and farther away a big, glass building which Antonio said was some Government ministry.

Manuel introduced Antonio and me to the students on the balcony, all terribly intense, some of them wearing beards like Castro. One of them was already spouting away into a microphone, making a dreadful din. Naturally I hadn't a clue what he was on about, and when Antonio tried to whisper what it was, I still wasn't any the wiser. I'm a bit of a nit about politics, I can't even follow them in England, let alone in Mexico, but Antonio had his arm round me while we stood there, and that was smashing. I'd got to the point you sometimes do with a person, when you need to have them with you all the time, you need to be touching them; you don't care how many people are look-

ing or what they might be saying, just as long as you've got
them beside you.

Of course I'd been getting a lot of niggling from the
British team, not so much from Marion and Joan now,
except for the odd dig, like, 'If they could only have her
chasing an electric Antonio, like a greyhound; she'd win by
streets!' but from some of the boys, especially in the restaurant, Latin lovers and all the rest of it, but funnily
enough it meant even less since that evening we made love
than it had before.

I think if Antonio hadn't been there beside me on the
balcony I'd have felt completely strange, completely and
utterly at sea, as far away from the people on the balcony as
I did from the people below, looking up at them. They were
like children, really, laughing and clapping; oceans and
oceans of them, these brown faces, stretching right back
across the square. I was glad when it got dark and it was
harder to see them; I could almost pretend we were there
alone, just me and Antonio.

When the helicopters came droning over, I didn't think
anything of it, they were just part of the whole strangeness.
Then all at once there was this great, green, dazzling light,
blinding you, like sheet lightning, then again, and suddenly
a bang, and then another bang, something going *whack*
against the wall, beside me; then someone screaming, a
woman, and Antonio grabbing me and pulling me to the
floor, coming down on top of me, bump, knocking all the
breath out of me, then more bangs, more screaming, and in
a flash it was all real, and I was terrified.

*The flares hung briefly in the dark like green fire, then, in the
moment that they vanished, came the shots, the first cries, prelude to a
crescendo of alarm in the square, the bewildered shouting and scurry-
ing of people stricken by some natural disaster, an earthquake or a
hurricane. The shots seemed, to those running, panic-stricken, for
shelter, to be coming now from the crowd itself, now from somewhere else. The roar and clatter of the helicopters heightened the*

61

chaos, but these, now, rose higher in the air and droned away from the square.

Most of the shots seemed to be aimed at the students' balcony, which had become an obscene shooting gallery, the row of heads above its parapet diminished first by one then by another, tottering and toppling like wooden, one dimensional effigies.

Then a new sound joined that of the bullets, the agonised yelling of the crowd; a sound of infinite, advancing feet, moving swiftly yet without haste, till soldiers burst into the square, invading it from every side, little, implacable Indians, the explosion of their rifles turning the syncopation of firing into a sustained, relentless percussion.

The soldiers went about their work with the devoted ferocity of hounds tearing a hare. They shot whoever they found in front of them; their rifles scorched and crimsoned the white shirts of boys, their bayonets drove into the backs of women, they killed and killed, as if the square was a slaughterhouse.

Here and there, at the whim of officers, prisoners were roughly taken, thrown into the back of trucks, then driven away. A bazooka roared; its shell hit the wall of the apartment block, beside the students' balcony, burst in an aureole of flame, which seared its way up to the roof.

There were no heads to be seen, now, on the balcony.

They were *firing* at us. God knows who, God knows why. I daren't look up, but the bullets seemed to be howling in from everywhere, I could hear them bouncing off the wall behind, hitting the balcony in front, I just screamed and screamed, I couldn't stop myself, till Antonio put his hand over my mouth. I had my eyes tight shut; then at last the bullets stopped for a few moments, and I heard voices shouting just above us, footsteps all around.

Antonio took his hand away and I opened my eyes very slowly, then I squirmed round and looked up; there were legs standing over us, I saw a man's hand in a white glove, holding a big revolver; behind me it sounded as if somebody was being dragged across the stone floor. Antonio yelled, '*Atleta, atleta!*' then the bullets came in on us again, *bang*, one just above my head, and I ducked right down, my nose was flat against the stone.

I don't know how long I stayed there, but it seemed forever. Somebody just near me gave an awful scream, they must have been hit, and I started to cry, it came pouring out of me, I was shaking and trembling and crying. Antonio held me tighter, but I shoved him away with all my strength.

Then, thank God, it all stopped, someone was pulling me to my feet; Antonio, I thought, and tried to break away, but it wasn't Antonio, it was a man I'd never set eyes on before, he seemed like a plain clothes policeman. Two more of them had hold of Antonio; one had a pistol pointed at his head; both of them were wearing white gloves.

They pushed and dragged us off the balcony, down the stairs, out of a back door, then shoved us against a wall. Antonio was pointing to his blazer badge and mine and saying, '*Atletas, atletas*', he looked white as a ghost, and then it all welled up in me, I started shouting at him, 'How could you bring me here? How *could* you, when you know I've got to run?'

Brian Glanville

The Mascot

Frozen in time and space, the cameo has the grotesque, paralysing horror of a nightmare. The figure, always absurd in its John Bull masquerade, a thousand times more absurd in the Mexican square, under the harsh sun, confronting the Mexican crowd, Union Jack raised high like a banner, transcending any question of courage in its blind assurance. But this time it was facing more than the apple cores of Cardiff, the hailstone whistling of the Romans. It was facing a vast explosion of hatred, chauvinism, mass resentment, its object summed up by the very flag it carried. So, to soundless fifes and drums, it marched ludicrously into the surge of threatening arms, hostile chants, like Moses into the Red Sea.

Mexico! Well, I thought to myself, there's an adventure, there's a challenge! My second World Cup, my tenth England tour, but of course I'd never ventured as far afield as this. Naturally it was a strain on the finances, that was why I didn't go to the Chile World Cup in 1962, but afterwards, I must confess, after the disappointment for England well, I felt a little guilty. I felt I *should* have been there, to give the lads just that little bit of something which they probably wouldn't get without me, not such a very, very long way from home. Seeing me there before the kick-off, with my Union Jack, wearing the old John Bull regalia; well, it's a little bit of England, isn't it? Of course it is. Especially when the crowd may not be friendly.

That time in Rome, the time they whistled me at the Olympic Stadium, I've never heard such a noise in my life, it really took me aback at the beginning, I thought it was going to split my eardrums. One of the players said to me afterwards, 'You've got a bit of guts, going out there on your own; at least there's eleven of us', but I never look at it like that. To me, it's a question of doing something for your country.

And really, you'd be surprised how nice foreign people can be. They respect you if you stick to your guns; throw your chest out, hold the flag high. *I'm* not ashamed of being English, and if that's old fashioned, then I'm glad to be old fashioned. That day at Wembley in 1966, the day England won the World Cup, was one of the proudest of my life. More than ninety thousand people in the stadium, and every one of them glad to be English. It was like Dunkirk all over again, or the Battle of Britain.

So I talked to Mother about it, and she was very good, as she always is. I told her I'd ask Mary, my widowed sister in Swanage, to come up and look after her, I'd put George, my manager, in charge of the two shops, and of course I'd write to her every day, as I always do. It would be expensive; I didn't hide that from her, even though I'd be on the charter tour, but she understood, she knew it wasn't just selfish pleasure.

'Mother,' I said, 'I only wish I could take you, too, you deserve a trip like that', but Mother's eighty-six now, and I'm afraid she's very nearly bed-ridden.

My passion for football. I've often seen it called that. Well, we're all mad about football, aren't we? Though my own sport was actually cycling, you may not know that. Oh, yes, I cycled for the county, I was even reserve for an international match, once, and I'm still honorary treasurer of the South Bedfordshire Cycling Association. But football's something you grow up with. I remember Ten Goal Joe Payne, when he was playing for Luton Town. I was there that day when he scored the ten against Bristol Rovers. Then after the war I got more and more interested in the England team. We had a lovely side then, of course – we have a lovely side now, too – Matthews and Finney and

Lawton and all those others. And in a way I suppose it was a consolation, because in those years we were being pushed about so much. Getting out of India. Getting out of Africa. The Mau Mau in Kenya. British soldiers being shot in Cyprus. It used to make me boil at times when I remembered the war, North Africa, the way they'd greeted us as we advanced through Italy. I thought, if only someone had the courage to go out and show the flag, people would believe in us again, because first we had to believe in ourselves.

It was a long time before I could put it into practice, I'm afraid. I had the business to look after, and there wasn't much money to spare, especially in the years when poor Father was dying. I went over to Belfast, that was the first time, and they received me very well there. Of course it isn't exactly foreign territory, they're very loyal to the Crown. In fact I only wish the football crowds everywhere in England would sing 'God Save The Queen' the way they do at Windsor Park. They were glad to see my Union Jack in Belfast. They cheered it.

Yes, I wore the John Bull outfit that day, too. I had it made for me to my design, the traditional design, and I generally expect to get through a couple of them a year. It seemed a natural choice to me. After all, what could be more British than John Bull? He's a symbol that's known all over the world. There's something stalwart about him and uncompromising. He stands for the days when nobody took advantage of Britain, days which I still hope will come back. As I said one day to some younger supporters, some of those long-haired ones, I don't see any disgrace in being proud of your country.

I've had many wonderful experiences since that first one. I've been all over Europe, waving my flag, and people have been marvellous to me. They've taken me into their homes, they've entertained me, even when we haven't spoken each other's languages. I walk through the streets in my little hard hat – they're made specially, too, at a good old Luton hatter's – with my Union Jack waistcoat, my knee breeches, and someone's sure to stop me for a chat, whether it's in

Stockholm or in Lisbon. I've made some really wonderful friends; some of them have been to stay with Mother and me, in London.

People say to me, 'You're always smiling', as if it surprises them, but why shouldn't I smile? Life's been very good to me. And I've always found that if you smile, people smile back at you.

Yes, he was always smiling. His smile had the fixed and painted quality of a puppet's, just as his face looked as if it had been carved perfunctorily out of wood, a gargoyle or a Mr Punch. He was too lean for John Bull, too convulsive, too anxious to please, making the imitation still more of a parody. His movements, too, were those of a marionette; he did not walk, he strutted. The ineradicable smile on his face, he marched jauntily around the football grounds, sometimes to the music of an actual band, always, even if the loudspeakers were vomiting 'pop', as if the band were there.

The smile, like his movements, was somehow less than human. It existed, not in response to anything, but almost in spite of everything, in its own right. His endless good humour resembled the detached benignity of a saint, a martyr. Go on, the smile seemed to say, spurn me, revile me, throw cans and apple cores and toilet rolls at me, I forgive you, I expect it. What is earthly pain when I know that I am going to my reward?

This flawed him utterly as John Bull, who surely never smiled, ingratiated or forgave. Perhaps this was why he never really emerged as the symbol of anything but himself, floating in the void, a cheer leader who raised no cheers, a standard bearer marching ahead of an army which had defected in the night. How could he arouse loyalty, passions, when he related to nobody?

In Guadalajara, where the England players in their shiny, pale blue tracksuits, sat endlessly around the hotel swimming pool, longing to bathe, wistfully looking at forbidden girls, he turned up one day in full attire, flag in hand, to wish them luck.

It was very hot, with the dry, implacable, torrid heat of Guadalajara. He had obviously conceived the occasion as a small ceremony. His movements, clockwork at the best of times, now seemed preconceived and ritualistic. Embarrassment hung in the hot air. He

67

smiled, smiled, his marionette's red cheeks sticky in the sunshine. 'Good luck!' he said to each player, saluting and shaking hands with him in turn. 'Best of luck!'

The players accepted his goodwill politely, with the wary tolerance of men confronting the afflicted. They did not smile, even covertly, at one another, nor, when he had gone, the last hand shaken, the last stiff salutation made, did they do more than exchange wordless looks, before going back to their cards, their conversation. He had come, he had gone, and had left no impression save a faint aura of surprise.

It was his imperviousness, perhaps, which guarded him as he went about Guadalajara, on his mission of mindless goodwill. For the city, which had welcomed the English players with its inevitable mariachi bands, the dark, balloon-cheeked, solemn men blowing and strumming, had been overcome by a wave of collective hatred. In default of the Americans, the eternal, oppressing gringos, the English would do, especially as the Brazilians were there to be juxtaposed and loved, with their samba chants, their gifts of flags and flowers.

The English were cold and aloof. Their manager would give no interviews. A bitter, bubbling sense of inferiority rose like a miasma out of the broad, hot, ugly streets and swirled around its prey. In the newly rebuilt Jalisco Stadium, rising in extravagant splendour outside the city, the crowd whistled the English team to scorn, whistled the name of every player as the loudspeakers announced it, each English kick, shot, and tackle when the games began. And through all this paraded the Mascot; smiling. Just as he had smiled, one remembered, that wet afternoon at Ninian Park, when the Cardiff crowd had pelted him.

Wales were playing England, and he'd set off before the game on his usual self-appointed lap of honour, raising his flag to the crowd on stands and terraces, smiling his inevitable smile. Then, as he'd turned a corner to pass in front of the terracing behind a goal, the bombardment began; pennies, apple cores, toilet paper, orange peel, a derisive shower of rubbish breaking about him as he went, his pace no faster, his flag held now like a flimsy shield.

After the terracing behind the goal, he had to face, moved to emulation, the long stretch of the popular side, the fusillade continuing, while he put it to shame with his indifference, his steady *step, and his unchanging smile. But that was Wales, and this was Mexico.*

For some reason they had it in for us, the Mexicans. If you ask me, there was envy at the bottom of it; that's what I've usually found. They seemed to take against us from the beginning, whistling our flag in the Aztec Stadium at the opening ceremony. I had some trouble with my own Union Jack a couple of times, once in the street in Guadalajara, where they tried to snatch it, once outside the Stadium, when they started spitting on it from up above. Really disgusting, that was; I don't often lose my temper but I had a job keeping it then, I can tell you. The other time, in the street, it was more of a joke than anything, just horseplay, young lads larking about. I managed to hold on to it, then I swung it round and round in a circle and got rid of them like that.

It's not often this sort of thing happens, though they like to have a go at me in Cardiff, I'm a regular Aunt Sally there, but I think it's just high spirits, really. I never miss a Wales–England game at Ninian Park. I have to show them that they can't beat me. Besides, it's usually just a minority that gets up to tricks like that, people in the main are good enough sports. I found that in Mexico, too; if you're friendly to them, they'll be friendly back.

Sometimes they'd stop me in the street and ask me, 'Why you don't like Mexico?' I'd tell them, 'But I *do* like Mexico. We *all* like Mexico. Why don't you like England?' Then they'd say because the English were proud, because they thought they were better than the Mexicans, and I'd tell them, 'We're better than everybody! But we respect everybody!'

In the stadium at Guadalajara they wouldn't let me on the pitch, but I stood among the other English supporters, waving my flag. The crowd whistled it, the people round us yelled at me and threw things, but I just went on waving. I'd come five thousand miles for this, and they weren't going to stop me now.

As time went on it got worse, the feeling towards us, till the worst thing of all, the night before our match against Brazil, when they made as much noise as they could outside the hotel to keep the players awake, right into the small hours. I've never been so angry in my life as when I heard about that, before the game started. I wished I'd known, I wished I could have been there, I'd have stood outside the hotel and appealed to them. I'd have said, 'You're sportsmen, aren't you? You want to keep up the good name of Mexico?' I believe the police just stood there and let them get on with it, which was disgraceful, let them prance about outside and drive round and round the hotel, hooting horns and shouting and screaming for Brazil, though hardly any of them were Brazilians.

People warned me that morning about going to the stadium in my John Bull clothes, they said it might be dangerous, but what had happened made me all the more determined. They weren't going to frighten *me*. I said, 'After all, look at what our boys have got to put up with. Running about in 98 degrees of heat, the whole crowd against them.'

And of course I had no trouble at all, just the usual whistling and a few things thrown at me inside the stadium. In fact afterwards, outside it, quite a few of them came up and spoke to me, they weren't unpleasant at all, they were very friendly, proving what I've said. I told them, 'What you people did last night was bad. It wasn't fair. You shouldn't treat your guests like that. When Mexico came to play in the World Cup in England, we treated them like gentlemen.'

Outside the towering, concrete stadium after the game, in the killing sun of early afternoon, one was surprised to see him cheerful and untouched, amongst a group of dark, friendly, smiling faces, the child in him appealing to the child in them. They touched his flag, admired his waistcoat, pointed wonderingly at his shining boots.

So he survived Guadalajara, and when the great, gaudy caravan of the World Cup moved into Mexico City, for its crescendo, one forgot about him. England's team had been knocked out, had gloom-

*ily gone home, and to that extent at least the anti-English emotions
had been gratified. Besides, who was there to vent them on now, in
all their vindictive glee?*

*He reappeared, obtrusively and unexpectedly, after the Final
itself. Brazil had won, and the huge, vertiginous bowl of the
Azteca Stadium throbbed with delight, a panorama of dappled,
sunlit colour, like an immense Dufy. Down on the green pitch, the
yellow shirt of a Brazilian footballer flashed here and there amidst a
welter of surrounding fans, leaping, dancing, gambolling in their
jubilation, now tearing the shirt off the black torso of some hero, now
hoisting him aloft on their shoulders.*

*It was a sight moving in its sheer, ingenuous joy, and into it,
irrelevant and uninvited, a silly spectre at the feast, strode the mascot,
smiling and insensible, his Union Jack in one hand, in the other, a
white placard inscribed in blue, ENGLAND CONGRATU-
LATES THE WINNERS.*

*At that moment, he was antipathetic, his intrusion, his self-
aggrandisement, lamentable. He had gatecrashed what in effect, for
all its public spectacle, was a giant family celebration. Yet there he
stood, jaunty as ever, bereft of any sense of solecism, giving his
smiling, jerky signals and salutes, which looked now like so many
nervous spasms. No one molested him. He might have been some
harmless imbecile, allowed to stand there winking and nodding like
an Aged Parent. After all, he meant no harm.*

After Guadalajara and all that went on there, I made up
my mind to one thing, I was going to give those Mexicans a
lesson in sportsmanship. I wanted to show them that even if
England *had* lost the World Cup, we knew *how* to lose, we
could still behave like sportsmen and appreciate the winning team, and what better way than to go out there on the
field in front of that whole great crowd, after the World Cup
Final, all the millions of people looking in on television, too,
and offer our congratulations, England's congratulations?

Getting permission wasn't easy. I had to talk to a lot of
people, members of our Football Association, and they had
to ask the World Cup Committee, but eventually I was told
I could, provided I only went on at the end.

It was a very proud moment indeed, a wonderful moment almost greater even than if we'd won the World Cup, again; I felt I was really representing England there. We might not have been playing in the match, but we were there at the end to say, 'Well done!' We'd invented the game, and by gum, we could still show everyone the spirit in which it ought to be played.

What an occasion it was, too, those great slopes towering up above you, the fireworks going off, balloons sailing up; oh, I wouldn't have missed it for a fortune. Yes, I was very proud that day.

Slowly and wearyingly, the coach had nosed its way out of the lee of the Azteca Stadium with its polyglot cargo of journalists; broad Russians, heavy Germans, tired English, a Dane or two, a Japanese. It made a bleak detour down narrow, muddy tracks, through a nearby shanty town, the tiny stone hovels topped, bizarrely, by a thicket of television aerials, crawled up the shabby serpent of the Insurgentes, to be becalmed at last on the fringe of that pullulating square.

It was then, from the beleaguered bus, as hands beat at the windows, faces leaped up and disappeared, like dervishes', feet kicked at the sides, that one saw him again, flag on high, ready to begin his crusade. In the sharp bathos of the moment, a phrase flashed into the mind: Dulce Et Decorum Est Pro Patria Mori. *Was this what he was seeking; a hero's death?*

One had no chance to follow the first impulse, leap from the coach and drag him inside, it was hemmed in beyond escape by the seething plethora of white shirts, straw sombreros and contorted faces. There was nothing to do but hope for him as he vanished into the maelstrom, swallowed up entire.

At Cardiff, when the apple cores flew round him, the journalists had said, 'Poor old bastard', yet one somehow felt his exhibitionism invited it. Now, as this crowd clambered on the cars and rocked the buses, screamed their chants of, 'Meji-co! Meji-co!' he was pitiable. What were his trivial shortcomings compared with this boiling up of senseless violence, of the brute nihilism forever pulsing in the streets?

It was more than an hour before the motor cycle police arrived in helmets and jackboots, the coach was extricated, and at last made off again, crossing the turbulent square, resuming the Insurgentes.

It was on the Reforma that suddenly one saw him, the march diminished to a limp, the hat gone, the flag torn and drooping. Through the coach windows, one could see him smile.

Janice Elliott

Block

He folded himself, like a dipped flamingo, to study more closely the gold tooth flashing at the back of her mouth. Cupping his hand to his ear, he dissembled deafness. There was something incredibly luxurious and wanton about that golden molar. He wondered if he could be a tooth fetichist. His wife, Judith, made love with her mouth shut, as if fearful of catching something. He did not know her teeth.

The thin girl had been standing on her own, alone but not apparently lonely. People glanced at her as they passed as if she were a statue. She had long pale hair which crossed in two disappointed wings beneath her chin. There was something blank and white about her, like a piece of paper. She looked surprised to be awake. He wondered if she might be drugged.

She repeated: 'It's a lovely party.'

He smiled, grotesquely he felt, lost for an answer, and as she closed her mouth experienced already a pang of nostalgia for that golden tooth. He said, if only to keep her talking:

'You like parties?'

'I like to watch.' She ran a finger round the top of her glass. 'Who are you?'

'I don't know.'

She nodded, as if this were a commonplace. He said, lost, but unwilling to lose her:

'You're too young to watch.'

'Oh me,' she smiled. 'There aren't many like me.'

People were strolling outside to the terrace. Someone swept between them. Then they too went outside. They looked through the hole in a greening bronze.

'What you need', she said, 'is someone to tell you who you are.'

The bronze (male? female?) had a lap. He sat on it. She settled neatly beside him. Its hermaphroditism redeemed an indecent act.

'I suppose that's why I came.' He crossed his legs and counted the things he had done today. He had woken at seven, extricated himself from Judith's arm which lay heavily across his chest (he had dreamed of angina pectoris), shaved, cleaned the kitchen, fed the older children, and left his wife. To what degree he had left Judith, he was not yet clear himself. In the flesh he might return, but the leaving, in his mind, had the certainty of a final act. He had passed the day in a state of curiously heightened perception (a brown dog outside college in Theobald's Road, the whiteness of his lunch-time salad). Having left the car for Judith, he went at the end of the day, the wrong way round on the circle line, to Karl's party.

She said: 'Male or female?'

'Simon Carter.'

'Paula. But I meant the sculpture.'

'Hard to tell.' He thought to the voyeur they must look intimate. A fat woman was throwing flowers into the swimming pool.

'Comfortable.'

She agreed. 'It must be female.'

'Why?'

'Haven't you noticed? Men don't have laps.'

He looked at his knees. Karl swam up. He was said to be incredibly gifted at pleasing women. Simon always thought of him as Levantine, in the sense that he chose to understand the word. He was soft and fat. He beamed at them over his breasts. Simon would have liked to tell him about his block. That was why he had come. He might tell Paula instead.

'Rather pretty, don't you think?'

'But what is it?'

Karl looked surprised. 'Does it matter?'

'I know,' said Paula. 'It's a hole.'

'It's what you make of it,' said Karl, and took Paula away. He steered her by a knobbly point at the top of her spine. She looked back at Simon and waved, regretfully he liked to think.

He gulped two whiskies from a trolley and walked over to the swimming pool. Karl's wife, Polly, laid a white padded paw on his arm. She was a female Karl. He imagined they fed one another with Turkish delight.

'Where's Judith?'

'The kids,' he said, vaguely.

'And you, Simon, you look tired? Working too hard?'

'The book. I can't get down to it. Hell, the truth is Pol, I've left her.'

Polly nodded. 'You should not go home. You should stay with us.' In the dusk Polly's face was a swimming disk. He felt so weak he might even stay. Polly thought Judith was a bad thing. 'She's a sweet girl. But she never understood.'

'No. You see, Pol, I couldn't *write*.'

She patted his arm again. 'You stay,' she said, 'you stay with us.' He wanted to explain.

'I'll think about it, Pol,' he said. He realized for the first time in five years he had known her as his publisher's wife, that she was a Jew. It made her, in a way that surprised him, less real. She waddled off and he thought he had forgotten to ask her about Paula.

He drank more. Some couples were dancing. By the pool a girl in a ginger wig (a man in a girl's ginger wig?) was singing softly to herself, finger on her lips, circling. She touched her breasts. No one noticed.

Simon found a poet he knew slightly and half-heartedly disliked, sitting under a tree with a bottle. They drank seriously and when the bottle was drained the poet swore softly and beautifully at great length. Simon realized he was expected to speak:

'I left my wife this morning. I am a teacher who can't teach. I have published two novels and now suddenly I can't write.'

'You gotta block.'

'Do you think so?'

'You don't feel real?'

'Oddly enough . . .'

'You gotta feel real. Before you write, you gotta know your name.'

'You're absolutely right! What I feel is . . .'

The poet lurched and for the first time looked directly at Simon. His expression was aggressive. He had ginger hair in his nose. Simon didn't like him again.

'You think you're someone special?'

'No. I . . .'

'You seen an analyst?'

'No.'

'What you want.' The poet was leaning so close Simon could have kissed him.

'Yes?'

'Is to get ironed out.' The poet was now patting him on the cheek. Simon felt cared for, justified in feeling that his effort in coming to this party would be rewarded by a message he had so far failed to receive. 'Like me.'

'I don't know your name?'

'Heybitch,' called the poet to the dancing girl, smiling and humming over them like a priestess: 'take this creep off my back.' Then he punched Simon, quite painfully in the stomach, and suddenly fell asleep.

Simon stood up for the lady, wobbling on his stalky legs. It was the girl who had danced by the swimming pool and unlike Paula, she was truly beautiful. He wondered he could ever have questioned her sex. She continued to weave in front of him, then kissed him. It was like a passing moth.

'My name's Simon,' he began.

'Hello Simon. I've got to swim.'

He followed her to the edge of the swimming pool. She handed him the ginger wig, or rather she threw it and he caught it like a bridesmaid. Then she plunged in, a beautiful dive, and sank at once to the bottom.

He found Karl and Paula. Karl, who seemed quite sober, was doing the talking while Paula nodded. They seemed, like everyone else, oblivious of the happening in the pool. Simon couldn't swim.

'There's someone in the pool.'

Karl waved his hand. 'There always is.'

Simon collected half a dozen people. They stood, very solemn, round the pool, some talking in low voices as if in Church.

'I tell you,' he said, 'she dived in and sank.'

'There's no one there.' The water was dark and closed. The flowers the fat woman had thrown still floated on the surface. The people became bored and began to mew for drinks.

Simon said: 'I've got her wig.' But he had dropped it somewhere.

Paula found him crying in the bronze.

'I was looking for you.'

'I thought you were with Karl.'

'He's fat.'

'That girl,' he said, 'she was really drowning.'

'You're dreaming,' said Paula, and climbed in beside him.

'Why have you got a gold tooth?'

'I haven't,' she said. 'It must have been the light.'

But in the womb of the sculpture he could feel her and she didn't seem to mind.

'It's been an awful evening.'

'Come on,' she said, as she sank down, in a marvellous, matter-of-fact sort of voice.

'You,' he had to ask. 'You're real.'

'I told you,' she said, 'it was female.'

As they left he felt sober, protective and loving. He steered her as far from the pool as possible. Something must have come to the surface. A crowd had collected.

'I'll see you again?'

'Oh yes,' she said, 'you'll see me again.'

The house smelled of babies and onions. He tripped on a toy in the hall and Judith called from upstairs. She was sitting up in bed watching television with the sound turned down. She looked handsome and competent and he wondered if he'd really left her. He started to undress.

'I went to Karl's party. I knew you wouldn't like it.'

She looked at him blankly. He sighed and settled on the edge of the bed. A young woman on the screen, half naked, appeared to be enjoying an orgasm. Judith ran her tongue lightly over her lips. There was something odd, and mysteriously familiar, about the girl's face. It was Paula.

'Who's that?'

She waited till the credits came up then, on a faint exhalation of breath, informed him: 'Paula Love.'

'It can't be. She was at the party tonight.'

'It was recorded,' said Judith, and pressed the knob to turn off the set.

In the dark he said:

'That can't be her real name.'

'I don't suppose it is.' A little later: 'You mean, you really haven't heard of Paula Love?'

'No.'

'What was she like?'

'She didn't seem all there. At first.' For a crazy moment he returned to his first hallucination, that it was Paula in the set, and at the party not Paula, but her shade or doppelgänger, a mysterious extension of Judith's goggle box. He wanted to tell her, as he would once have told her, easily without shame, of his deepest fantasies. He touched her double nylon thigh, but she misunderstood:

'I haven't got my cap. And I've taken a pill. Besides, you're pickled.'

'Sorry.'

But later:

'Simon?'

'Mmm?'

'I was a bit foul. Sorry. I was fed up. I had a silly idea, all day, you'd gone for good.'

He laid a hand on her pleasant rump and patted it twice.

'Go to sleep.' But she was already unconscious and snoring softly.

He got up, crept downstairs to his desk and began to write:

"He folded himself, like a dipped flamingo, to study more closely the gold tooth flashing at the back of her mouth."

Then he wrote, high up at the top of the page:

BLOCK

Janice Elliott

Hymeneal

Susan Edden, just married, comes to the farm in 1921. Up the hill, but down in status, according to her mother, the doctor's wife. She has spent her life on the edge of, but never in farms. She comes up with Jesse ('Jesse', her mother says, 'sounds like a girl. Is that a name for a man?') in the cart, not her father's car. Starting, she says, with a crispness that comes naturally to her, as she means to go on. But really because she fancies it.

Even outside the church, the two families keep to themselves. Eddens stiff and sweating in tight best suits; Aitkens moving easily in their clothes, capturing the vicar. Kisses, handkerchiefs, tears, some Aitken confetti, then suddenly, miraculously, from the Edden side great boughs and branches of orange blossom and lilac, spread at their feet, piled in the cart. Jesse swearing and blinking behind flowers. Joe, father Edden, missing, then up the road comes a flowering bush, swaying, almost a tree, all white. It seems a long time coming. The light shakes. Then, shedding some flowers, it is tumbled across their laps into the cart. And Joe colours and winks, first one eye, then the other, and just as embarrassing remarks and damp farewells seem inevitable, he thumps the mare, like a barmaid, on the backside, and she shivers, farts and leads off.

Someone has stuck cow-parsley in the mare's harness and hung two little bells on the reins. The white dusty blooms tickle her ears. It is a light cart. She trots and the bells ring. Between the village and the bare hill there is a natural avenue of bushes and trees. They move under white haw-thorn, between high green, on their throne of boughs. Susan leans against her husband's shoulder. He puts an arm round her, leaving one hand for the reins.

'It was a lovely idea,' she says, and when he seems not to understand: 'the flowers.' Inside her head her voice sounds artificial, patronizing. She would like to swallow her words, but no harm is done. He seems wrapped in some dream of his own. He is a small, brown, slim man, his only weakness, it appears to her, a shyness at having snatched her from the arms of suitable young men. She must reassure him. She blesses, for once, her intelligence, which will find a way to convince him of her love, his own worth.

He grunts: 'They'll want a do.'

'Yes,' she says, 'of course. They'll expect it. For them.'

'And you. It would be right.'

'Oh, me. I don't care about things like that.'

'You're a funny one.' For the first time since they were married, half an hour ago, he really looks at her, puzzled and loving. 'You know what you're in for? What you've lost?' He touches her cheek.

She laughs, clear-throated, easy. So that's what bothers him.

'If you knew ... how boring those people are. What you've saved me from.'

'Perhaps.'

'Hurry,' she says, 'hurry. I want to begin.' They are out of the avenue and there is the hill and the house. She wants to throw open the windows, bring in flowers. The horse stops trotting and plods. 'Make her go fast.' She is excited and wants to tease him. 'Or don't you whip mares?'

'Oh yes,' he says. 'They're all the same, beasts.'

She likes to see him so sure with the reins. Something her father could not do. She congratulates herself on her instinct in choosing this man. She wishes only that she could spark off the same excitement in him. He kisses her softly on the cheek and touches the mare with the whip. They trot up the hill, shedding flowers.

The yard is smaller than she remembers, the ugly black barn bigger. A skinny dog runs out and barks at them. He swears gently and it retreats, after a moment's doubt, wagging and cursing, back to its place under the barn.

'No, he says, 'the front door.'

They go through the side gate, stiff, never used, to the front of the house. He has to kick the hinge. Between the house and the hedge there is half an acre of freshly turned earth. He is proud of this and shy. She knows that she must look pleased, though it's hard to imagine, at this moment, what she might do with it. He points to the boundaries. He has spent every evening in the last month, from nine to eleven, digging.

'There! That's yours. Your garden.' Anxious: 'You like flowers? You said?'

'Yes,' she says, and kisses him. 'Thank you. I love it.' Love, lovely, seem the only words she can say today. They don't mean much. They have been rubbed flat of meaning. But he doesn't notice. He uses words as the nearest tools that come to hand, rough and ready. Some fresher for his simplicity. She tells herself, I must go carefully; show him but not spoil him. She talks about roses and they go in.

She serves the cold chicken, puts away clothes and arranges her books. She can see how she might make this house her own, in time, with tact. Her mother caught her packing the books and said: 'You'll have no time for them.' 'Then I'll make time.'

'Your reading,' he murmurs, touching their spines as if they held secrets. 'I can hardly read more than my name.'

'I'll teach you if you like.'

'If there's time. Yes. I'd like that.' He looks at her in wonder. 'You're a queen, you know.'

She smiles. She is entirely happy and convinced of the rightness of her choice. 'But you too. You can do things I know nothing about. I'll be a fool, I know, on a farm. You'll have to show me.'

'You'll learn.'

After they have drunk tea (she would have preferred

Janice Elliott

coffee but the tea, after all, tastes right) they go up. There is no electricity here, or gas. She is enchanted by the low roofed room and the oil lamps. She turns them down and waits in the dark. She thinks he will be shy. He smells of soap.

'You've shaved.'

'Yes.'

'Kiss me.'

They have kissed often. This is familiar. She likes it, would like to prolong it. She feels very powerful, able to please him.

'Don't stop.' He pauses, propped above her on one elbow. His voice is baffled, almost resentful.

'Why did you marry me?'

She refuses to take him seriously. 'Now ... let me see.'

'Not my money or my looks.' He is still solemn, quite stern. 'Nor my reading. Was it a fancy?'

'Jesse! What do you think I am?'

'I think you're a clever young woman, who, if choice were hers, would maybe never marry. Not as clever as you think. And you'd not be as content alone as you'll imagine, in bad times.'

She is touched by his seriousness. 'We'll have no bad times. I know it. Or none we can't overcome.'

He seems not to have heard her.

'And you wanted to do something with yourself. You've got pride in yourself. But you didn't know what. Just that it had to be something the others don't do. You might have gone to one of those universities, been a teacher. But you fancied me.'

'That's a terrible thing to say!' She is near to tears. They are whispering as if in Church. She had thought she held him, quiet and small, in the palm of her hand.

'No. For most that's what it comes down to, fancies. All I say is, Susan, don't build on me, not too much. That is, you can count on me always, I hope. But don't think I can be owt but myself.'

'I don't understand!'

'It doesn't matter. It was best said now.' He smiles and pulls her hands away from her eyes. Then he begins to laugh and romp like a young dog. He fools about, and kisses and tries to be gentle, but it still hurts, more than she could have believed possible. At once, he falls asleep. She lies awake, hurt and bewildered. He takes her once more in the night, without even opening his eyes. This time it is better. But her wedding night is not at all what she expected.

The next three days – a long weekend – are good. The farm is still small. It will grow in the next forty years, but now it is possible for Jesse to take a short holiday. Through the four-day honeymoon an Edden cousin and another man keep things going but avoid the house, averting their eyes as they follow their sloped shadows across the yard when, in the early morning, woken by unfamiliar farm noises, Susan appears at the window.

'There's Tam. I think I've shocked him.'

He plunges his head in the bowl, pokes soap out of his ears.

'Not Tam. He thinks you're Queen of England.'

'And you?'

'I'll show you what I think. Give me that towel.'

'I might and I might not.'

He lunges after her, blind with soap, groping. 'You're a skinny cat.'

She sidesteps. Wherever she goes, he follows, but slow, threatening and swearing, roaring. It's like having a blind bull on a chain. They are behaving like children. This is the best time they will have.

'Give.'

'Say I'm the Queen of England.'

'I'm boggered if I will.'

He pins her down at last and wipes his eyes on the sheet. These are silly, private jokes. Instinctively, from a sensibility with which she does not credit him, he gives her all the non-sense she wants, but does not know she wants. She may deny later, even to herself, that she has ever been so frivolous. She has gone into this marriage, she likes to think, with her eyes open, determined that it shall be good and lasting: she sees them as reasonable friends, teaching each other. He will learn to read, to listen to music (for which she feels he has a natural, if untutored ear); she to be a farmer's wife. Concerning the second project she is vague but optimistic. She has always been competent. As for his education, that will be a matter of tact and patience and love. Their marriage will be all the richer – out of the ordinary – for these mutual benefits. She brings a great if invisible dowry and has a brain clear enough and a temperament cool enough ('Susan is such a *sensible* girl') to bestow it without offence or patronage. This is how her mind runs. She prizes her mind more than her looks. On one subject she might admit she is a romantic – common sense.

In these four days – after that first, odd night – her sensible resolutions are blurred by happiness. She notices, on the fourth day, that he is restless. His hands on the fine tablecloth (her mother's present) look foolish and empty. He wants to get back to work.

'You're worried about the farm?'

'The lambing's started. Tam's no shepherd. We can't afford to lose them.'

'Shall we go and see?' She has noticed the pen in the sloping field behind the house, up in the corner, where the hedge makes a windbreak.

'You wouldn't mind?'

'I'd like to.'

'You're a good girl.'

'No. I'm just your wife. Besides – ' she adds, with something of her natural airs – 'I've never seen an animal born.'

'It might be best if you stayed.'

'No. I want to come. If I won't be in the way?'

'You' he says, and touches her cheek, 'you.'

They walk up the hill hand in hand. Up here there is a wind and the stars seem to be running, racing, falling. The couple pause for breath and look up:

'It's fine' he says.

'Yes. It's lovely. You know them?'

'No. Only the Plough.' He jabs his thumb where the stars seem windiest. 'And the Milky Way. Tam knows them. He's learned them from fishing.' She knows what he means but likes to imagine Tam, sturdier and blacker than his cousin, monosyllabic, drawing in his trawling net great shoals of stars. She doesn't mention this. It sounds like the fancy of a silly girl. She frowns, as if dazzled, and says, offhand:

'It's strange to think some of them are dead. We're seeing them but they're not really there. You can think of space but not time. At least you can, but separately. Not time in space.' Walking with her face tipped up she catches her ankle in a root. He holds her and they go up.

Tam has a lantern in the pen. A ewe lies on her side, apparently dead, but as they watch, the stomach, grossly extended between four skinny legs, heaves and flutters. The green eye of the sheep, still open, seems to observe them. Tam nods:

'I was coming down. But by the time I found her she was near finished.'

'She's gone?'

'Aye.'

'When?' Jesse looks angry. For a second Susan thinks that he might strike Tam.

'Now. A minute. Two maybe.'

'Knife.'

Tam blinks. 'You're going to cut her?'

Jesse has already flung off his coat and is kneeling. He nicks the ewe's belly, then remembers Susan:

'You'd better go back to the house.'

'Can't I help?'

'It'll need feeding, if it lives, till we can find it a ewe. Warm some milk.'

But she stays. Tam holds the lantern and she watches the two men, heads bent. She feels a fool, useless, but is too interested to leave. Then she is appalled as the womb is revealed and Jesse plunges his hands deep in like a woman in dough and pulls out the bloody mess. It's foul and marvellous. He's smiling. She stuffs her knuckles in her mouth and staggers outside to be sick. When she has finished she stays hunched, her cheek against the prickly black grass.

'I told you, get back to the house.' His voice is rough. He keeps his soft face for the lamb. She follows him down the hill.

'How will you get another ewe to take it?'

'Find one with a dead lamb. Skin it. Put the skin on this 'un.'

She stumbles but his arms are full with the lamb. She feels absurdly lonely, excluded, and then is ashamed of herself. Her voice sounds high and artificial:

'You did it so quickly. You seemed to know just what to do.'

'I'd better, it's my job.'

'But I'd have no idea ...'

'It's what you know. Nothing special. Like your reading.'

'But that seems so pointless. It doesn't do anything for anyone but myself. It doesn't save a life.'

'A life?' he says. 'Don't go romancing about it. It's only a beast. I'd kill it as quick for money.' But his face is slanted away from her, towards the sheep, now kicking in his arms. 'You little bogger then, you want to run?' He sets it down and it wobbles in a circle back to him. 'I'm not your mam.' He picks it up again and now they're back at the farm. He says they'll keep it indoors for the night. It's sickly but should live. The honeymoon is over.

She stays outside for a moment in the yard. The racing sky makes the barn topple. There is a scent of hay and salt. She looks up, breasting the waves of darkness, to the high corner of the field where the stars are low and in the pen the lantern glows, a single small outpost of humanity in a scene suddenly cold and by no means benign. She shivers and goes indoors to warm the milk.

Janice Elliott

The Noise from
the Zoo

From where he dug in the night Felix could hear the zoo.
As the last visitor left the murmur began; these were the
smaller, familiar animals, the gossips, but by midnight the
larger and the rarer gave voice and Felix paused to listen
to the bellows, moans of complaint, and wild laughter.
At first this seemed to him an hysterical conversation between insomniacs, later, as weariness and fancy overtook
him, the Passion of the beasts, the desperate cry of martyred
innocents. He did not care for zoos. The animals appeared
to him prisoners without hope of release or redemption.
Those not captured but born there were like the blind born
without sight. For himself, if he were a beast and could
choose he would prefer capture, if only to have something
to remember, to talk about at night.

He rested a while and opened his sandwiches and flask.
A policeman loomed out of the dark. Felix held his breath.
The policeman took in the dim red lamp, the shovel, and
the low barricade around the growing hole.

'Fine night for it. On your own?'

Felix nodded and offered him coffee. They drank. The
policeman walked on. First he looked over the barricade:

'You've got a good hole there.'

When he had finished Felix tidied up, took the shovel but
left the barricades and the lamp. Eventually someone
would probably take them away. Meanwhile the hole was
deep enough but not so deep a running child or an unwary

adult falling in, might harm themselves. That was important. That was part of the plan, just as it was to Felix of no
significance that the hole would sooner or later be filled in.
He hurried home and at seven o'clock woke his wife, Audrey,
with a cup of tea.

Audrey said for the tenth time: 'What do you mean, a
hole?'

Her brother, Gerald, shifted the pipe in his teeth. 'He
means what he says, Aud. A hole.' He drew in to the kerb
and parked. He added: 'Is a hole.'

'That's what I meant,' said Felix.

The hole had not yet come to official notice, or if it had,
was assumed to be to some public purpose. The lamp and
the barricades declared its right to be there. It was a fine
Saturday morning in the Park. Some women were sitting
by the hole in deckchairs. They called to their children to
come away from the edge. A tramp spat in the hole. A
couple of girls laughed at it. Audrey looked at it sideways,
not to be caught out. Gerald planted himself in front of
it.

'It's quite a small hole.'

'It's big,' said Audrey sharply, 'it's far too big.'

Gerald twinkled: 'Too big what for?'

'Don't encourage him,' she snapped. 'He's mad.'

'Well,' Gerald repeated, turning to Felix, 'what for?'

'Nothing.'

'Why?'

'For no reason.' Felix averted his eyes from the hole. He
was determined that it should be pointless. If he looked too
long he might be moved by it, was aware already of stirrings
of pride as people paused to peer in.

When they got back to the car Audrey was waiting, tense,
ready to cry. At home, without Gerald, who had gone off
laughing and wagging his head, she turned to Felix:

'How can you do a thing like that for no reason? Are
you mad? What do you hope to gain by it?'

'Nothing.'

'Then what? Do you *want* to get into trouble?'

'Certainly not.'

She gave him a wild, white look and began to sob. 'If you wanted a hole you could have had one *here*!'

He was disturbed, troubled for the first time since he thought of the hole. He began to see the danger. He spread his hands: 'Don't you see, it wouldn't have done? Here, in our garden, where we live, it would have meant something? It would have had a reason, a consequence. The essence is its pointlessness, that is its beauty.' He pondered, got himself a beer and took it into the garden. He had chosen a hole because it was empty, meaningless, the perfect, motiveless act. Yet already the policeman had described it as good, Audrey said it was big, Gerald small. He himself had spoken of beauty. He wondered. For the first time he cared for the hole, wished to run and protect it from corruption, interpretation. It would be better it should be filled, even that. He hurried to save his hole.

He took a risk, going in daylight. He had thrown in only half a shovelful of earth when authority, at last awakened, tapped him on the shoulder.

'I didn't want to hurt anyone. I don't believe in violence. I wanted to prove something.'

'?'

'That an act is possible, in itself, without motive or consequence. The relief of something pure that couldn't be spoiled. Objective, without past or future. I have a good job. I love my wife. She had nothing to do with this.'

The hole was not at once filled in. It became at first somewhere to go on a bright evening where the children could play, then a kind of shrine. Larger barricades were put up because of the danger that the walls might cave in. The police measured it. It appeared on television. People began to throw in flowers, even coins. They stood around in knots as if they expected something to happen. It became a famous spot for harmless lunatics, preachers and lovers.

Those who questioned Felix were inclined at first to be lenient, to dismiss him as a harmless nut. He was consistently calm and polite, was revealed through investigation to have been, up to now, an entirely respectable citizen, modestly ambitious, reasonably successful. And after all, it was only a hole.

The Inspector considered himself a bit of a liberal. He had met most sorts and while it was his job to bring them to book he had experienced, more than once, a twinge of sympathy for the anti-social. He admitted to Felix:

'These youngsters, they're not the only ones who can't stomach what's going on. Your conformist society. Your welfare state.' He twinkled. 'There are times when I've felt like chucking a brick myself. We've had most things, but I must admit we've never had a hole.'

Felix smiled. They had several such one-sided conversations. The weather grew hot. The Inspector sweated. He was aware of neglecting his other duties. He became obsessed with the hole. He dreamed of it as a vacancy into which he might fall. He walked with his eyes cast down. He was afraid to sleep.

It was August, the silly season. In other parts of London holes began to appear overnight. Some revealed subterranean streams, archeological remains, or the bones of those who had died by violence in war or by stealth. Some, like Felix's, were empty.

Felix's case came up, he paid a small fine. The magistrate asked if a psychiatric report had been made. It had. Felix was sane. But for the mysterious notoriety the hole had achieved, this would have been the end of the affair. As he left the court Gerald took his elbow:

'You'd better duck into the car double quick.' A quarrelsome crowd had gathered. A man carrying a placard inscribed KEEP THE HOLE was hit by a tomato. A woman screamed. The police arrived to break them up and Felix slipped away unobserved.

'I never meant this to happen.' Felix explained that evening to the Inspector. The Inspector arrived on foot, in civilian clothes. He looked unfamiliar, as if he might be wearing a disguise, and very tired. They sat in deckchairs in the garden and drank beer.

'If you could explain it,' said the Inspector. 'If you could say you were looking for something.'

'I wasn't.'

The Inspector nodded glumly.

'If you had buried something or heard of something buried . . .'

'No.'

The Inspector sighed.

'I have dreams.'

'You need a holiday.'

Felix had grown to like the Inspector. He wished he could help him.

'Now look here, old chap,' said Gerald, 'this has got to stop. It's making Aud ill. Enough is enough.'

'It's out of my hands,' said Felix. That night he was woken by her crying. He touched her shoulder but she curled away, drawing her knees up to her chin. She had grown thin and her shoulders were sharp. The bones cut her flesh like knives. At last she said:

'I don't see why you had to do it. You had everything.'

'It is the only thing I have done in my life.'

'But it has brought nothing but trouble.'

'It has been misunderstood.'

They lay for a while, before they slept, fingers touching in the dark.

The Inspector had got into the habit of calling most evenings. When he appeared Audrey shut herself in the kitchen. As they paced the garden she watched, a pale, wavering shape in the window.

The Inspector looked at the lettuces.

'You've never thought, there might be a reason, something you've forgotten? The kind of thing the trick cyclists dig up?'

'No.'

The Inspector shook his head. 'I go along with them

Janice Elliott

there. I've read a bit. Everything we do has a motive. What do you see in the hole?'

'Nothing.' As if to reassure himself Felix repeated: 'nothing.'

As he left the Inspector said:

'Had you heard? They're going to fill it in.'

The workmen sent by the Parks Committee to fill it in were met by a hostile crowd. A Save the Hole group had been formed and this demonstration was clearly well organized. Some carried placards bearing Felix's picture and the slogan: AN ENGLISHMAN'S HOLE IS HIS CASTLE. Some had actually climbed the barricades and settled in the hole with sandwiches. The police arrived. There was a scuffle. The squatters in the hole refused to budge and the police did not bother to lift them out. After all, it was only a hole. The workmen retreated.

That night there was a torchlight procession. Each hole was visited from the City through Pimlico to Chelsea then north to the Park. They sang quietly as they marched and Felix watched with fear and wonder as they approached, the brands flickering among the trees. Leading them was the Inspector, wild-eyed, his head thrown back like a prophet. He did not see Felix. His gaze was fixed on the point where, from the direction of the zoo, the police came with shovels.

The marchers tore down the barricades. No one ever knew who threw the stone but it hit the Inspector on the temple. With a look of surprise he swayed and toppled into the hole. Fights broke out. A passing and oblivious dog, his mind perhaps on burying bones, paused, was astonished by the hole and set up a piercing howl. From the zoo a hyena answered. One man seized a brand and set fire to his clothing. Then a fine rain, the first for weeks, began to fall.

When the crowd had been dispersed and the injured carried away Felix, who was not the kind of man you would notice in a riot, came out from the trees and stood by the hole. He hardly recognized it. In the fighting the edges had been broken and it had already begun to fill with rain.

94

He saw it, thinking of the Inspector, as a grave; soon it would be a pond. If you looked long enough you could make anything you liked of it. Someone had left a lamp. Kneeling, the rain trickling down his neck, he held it close to the rising surface of the water and saw, reflected, a face he recognized to be his own. He stood, awkwardly, and found that he was crying. He stayed for a while listening to the noise from the zoo.

Janice Elliott

Interview

'So what would you do next? Normally, I mean.' The young man was very tall. He walked around the low-beamed cottage. When he paused to make a note or ask a question his pale cotton trousers rode up revealing celery legs. He settled in high places where no one had ever sat before.

'I'd work, I suppose,' she said, then with more confidence 'I write every morning from ten till two.'

'Splendid!' said call-me-**Sim**on, as if she were a clever child. 'We'll do that.'

'Won't it be a bit dull?'

'Not if we do voice over. But leave that to us.'

'Oh.'

She sat at her desk. She pulled in the chair, put paper in the typewriter and raised her hands. Outside her husband was mowing the lawn, round and round. He was being considerate, she knew, making himself not there. She suspected that call-me-Simon thought Bill was the gardener, and could imagine no way, short of the farcical, of putting this right.

Her face was stiff with smiling. 'I can't think what to write.'

'Just behave normally. Pretend we're not here.' The camera whirred.

She lit a cigarette from the box which was also kept filled on her desk, remembered she had a small pride in not smoking on television ('I don't know why but I can't stand women puffing on the box'), squeezed it out, tipped it into the wastepaper basket and pushed the dirty ashtray in a drawer. She waited for the wastepaper basket to burst into flames. She tried to stop smiling but couldn't. Perhaps she would be stuck for life with this idiotic grin. The camera prowled closer, an enquiring bird. I am a watchbird watching you.

She typed: THE BROWN FOX JUMPED OVER
THE
Janet Johnson
Well Cottage
Wishing Green
Janet Craig-Cooper is a lazy dog

'It's silly,' she said, 'I can't think what to write.'

The camera retreated, respectful but implacable, waiting. Janet looked at Bill through the double-glazed picture window. He had finished going round and round. Now he would mow the edges. He made a point of not looking at her. He encouraged her work. He said it was important. Once or twice he had been called Mr Johnson. Janet Johnson wrote cool, intelligent novels about women with domestic problems. Her own life ran so smoothly. She led Simon round the house, showing him, 'That was the bread oven,' she said. 'This is the original fireplace and that's Jacobean. That's my husband out there and this is Matthew.'

'Marvellous,' breathed Simon, 'marvellous.'

Matthew was conservative. He did not approve of anything that was happening today. Such a pity, Janet often said to Bill, that the nearest play group was ten miles away. Someone younger to cope with him, an au pair perhaps? But more trouble than they were worth and hopeless in the country. And then he adored Mrs Munnery and next year he'd be at school. A nanny, of course, was out of the question. Mrs Munnery was one thing, but to hand over your child body and soul to another was a treachery Janet could not even consider.

She stooped but Matthew would not come to her. He told Simon: 'I'm four. I was sick last night.'

Simon said it would be absolutely marvellous if they could get a shot of Janet bathing Matthew. He had already been bathed, as usual, by Mrs Munnery when she came in at nine, but now Janet was to bath him again. The idea was so utterly absurd that the vague hysteria which had been rising in her all day nearly broke out. But she was carried away on a tide of arrangements, proposed by Simon. She felt helpless, strangely isolated in her own house, awkward with her child.

Matthew did not care to be bathed. He protested, was bribed and cajoled and finally gave way, but held himself resentfully stiff. He captured the soap and with a foxy smile cracking a face she felt to be varnished, Janet urged him: 'Give the soap to Mummy, Mat.'

Janet sweated. Simon asked from his perch on the lavatory: 'Can you tell us what you are working on now?'

'Give the soap to Mummy, Mat, at once.'

'What do you feel about the future of the novel?'

'Matthew, GIVE ME THE SOAP.'

Simon said vodka. Oh well, yes, then he'd just have a tonic. The crew had gone down to the pub. Janet's hand was shaking. She poured herself a double whisky. She waved to Bill who was squatting on the lawn in the midst of the dismantled mower, happy as a child on a beach. He looked straight at her, it seemed, but did not wave back; it would be the angle of the light. Help! she wanted to cry and gulped half her whisky before she turned to Simon. 'I'm not much good at this, I'm afraid. I didn't really want to do it.'

'Of course you didn't. It's irrelevant.'

'So you do understand!'

Janet Johnson made Janet Craig-Cooper do it. Janet Johnson agreed with her publisher and her agent and her husband that this was just the kind of breakthrough she needed to reach a wider public. Since Janet Craig-Cooper was proud of Janet Johnson she consented, admitted even, with a part of her mind, that she wanted madly to do it. Writers and such who despise sales figures and pull up the drawbridge against opportunities like this, were simply not living in the world. After all, one was writing to communicate, or one should be or one should not be writing at all. I mean one can live in an ivory tower and chuck whisky bottles at call-me-Simon, but might that not imply that one has nothing to say, or worse still, something to hide?

Janet Craig-Cooper knew that everything was not only under control but as good as it could be: happy, healthy child, placid husband, full fridge, poulet au blanc and Gewurztrauminer for Simon and Janet Johnson, nothing to do but whisk off the covers and serve.

'Oh well yes of course I've thought about giving it up when Matty was born for instance I wish I could sometimes be like ordinary women if there is such a thing it must be heaven but. Honestly, I think and Bill agrees I'm much nicer if I'm working and being Bill I can't imagine a situation in which I would have to choose Bill says. Of course one's family first if Matty were ill but well yes, one does hope that never.

'Sometime perhaps though Bill doesn't feel strongly and I. I have no intention of disclosing to several million indifferent ears the obstetrical details of a perfectly hideous confinement. I couldn't write when I was pregnant, it's quite common. I hated it, I hated Matthew for the first six months of his life. Janet Johnson out in the garden eating worms while Janet Craig-Cooper grew fatter and madder. Not for your box.

Yet I dream sometimes of the girl even Bill doesn't know about this. If Matty died endlife. Endwork? I truly don't know. Don't ask. Don't look. If Bill.

'Oh yes, Bill is really marvellous, he's so patient. How women manage with a husband who doesn't *understand*. I'm lucky, I know I'm lucky.'

Janet Johnson told a funny story about the only time she and her husband had a row about her writing. He said something wasn't quite up to her best and there'd been this fantastic scene though of course he was quite right, as she realized even at the time which was why she threw the casserole on the floor. And there they were on their knees mopping up pot roast then picking bits of glass out of one another's hands then they both saw the joke.

Janet Craig-Cooper remembered it had not been so funny although it happened exactly as she said. She remembered she had tried to conceive that night or rather not tried not to conceive; and had gone through hell for three weeks thinking she might actually have brought it off. That was Matthew.

The rows we have not had since are the dark places in our marriage where we do not go.

'Marvellous,' said Simon, 'you restore my faith in marriage. The new book?' An autistic child, the strains on the parents, weak father, divided mother, you know the thing. ("To a potentially melodramatic situation Miss Johnson brings her customary subtlety of perception, honesty and wit. All the more moving for the restraints imposed by a formidable intelligence, the compassionately forensic revelations of a writer who is never afraid to plumb the darker, most private corners of human experience.") Have you ever tried to plumb a corner, for God's sake?

'Actually, I did do a bit of research. Those children, you know, it's terribly sad. I felt awful, like a spy.' I sat in on classes for autistic children for exactly one day, after which I drove home very fast and was sick as a dog who's been eating dirt. I did my Belsen wardress act with Matty. By the time Bill came in I was howling, he was so sweet. How could I tell him I was howling for poor Janet who can't see anything nasty without throwing up?

Janet writes about nasty things because she doesn't want to look at them. Writing sends them away. When she had nightmares as a child she used to draw pictures of the monsters then she would stamp on the pictures and tear them up.

If Matty died end Janet so Janet Johnson kills children on paper paper children to placate the gods.

'I can't imagine what use you can make of this. I'm a very ordinary person.'

At lunch Janet was benevolent, smiling at the head of her table flanked by the two men. Having never before given an interview in her own home, at such indulgent length, she was now drunk with the urge to self-exposure. She could say anything and millions would bend their ears: more than ever read her books. Bill this is Simon Judd, my husband Bill. Call me Simon. Bill smiled, squeezed her shoulder in the kitchen. Well done. It's going well. Your wife's a perfect woman, Bill. I know. Perfect poulet au blanc, sauce not too thick, I say what a super wine.

'The beams were plastered in the most frightful cream paint. It took us months to strip.'

Matty off for his rest. Hug Matty. Bye-bye, love.

'All this . . .'

'Well, we like it, don't we darling.'

Window open, warm air, bee among the roses. Commuting, converting cottages, living in the country. Telly. Scandalous tales from Simon who is after all rather sweet. Certain lady author who tried to seduce him.

'Not *her*? But I thought . . .'

'Apparently not.'

'Coffee?'

'The most frightful things! They start all uptight about telly then they forget, poor dears, and out it all comes, the lot, you'd never believe. The yards of film we waste. I ought to be a priest, no?'

'Brandy?'

'But it's perfect here. I could stay here forever.'

'Of course writing is very lonely. However understanding your family are, you're on your own.' Janet Johnson, slightly tight, imagines sleeping with call-me-Simon who is paid to be absolutely riveted by every word she says. An illusion, of course, she knows, but she is disarmed. Janet Craig-Cooper accepts a kiss from her husband who is going to put the mower together again. Nice meeting you, see you later. Goodbye, Bill.

This is the crunch, formal interview face to face before

watchbird camera which through lunch was hooded beneath a black cloth, now waits. Simon is male nurse, big brother, lover and priest. Very gentle. 'I'll just ask you a few dull questions and you say what you like. We can always cut. Smoke, drink, do a strip if you like. Just be yourself.' Who?

Some technical stuff about light meters and sound. Trouble about sibilance. Just say something.

'I'm terribly sorry, I can't think of anything to say.'

'OK, Stan?'

Thumbs up from Stan.

'All systems go.'

Intro from Simon, blah about talented young author, sixth novel, one of the best women novelists writing today, also wife and mother. Own life so clearly er-happy, er-content, striking contrast between author herself and the deeply disturbing questions she poses which challenge the foundations of our everyday lives. Janet?

Outside, through the double glazing, Matty is trundling a wooden horse round the pond. Mrs Munnery will be washing up. Matty and Bill are discussing the mower like old men. The continuity man is reading Bill's Yachting World. The room is full of cables and heavy, breathing strangers, only Simon familiar, head cocked sympathetically for Janet Johnson.

'Can you tell us, perhaps, how you arrive at these themes? Is there an er conscious motivation on your part?'

'Fear. I am frightened all the time. When I was a child I was frightened of dogs.'

No more than a flicker of alarm on Simon's professional face. This was an easy job, a rather dull, sensible female who wrote reasonable books that were supposed to be terribly perceptive, his secretary said. A good cook too.

Pity. She's off again.

Smile for the camera. 'You see I'm frightened of death, of my husband dying, or Matty, or me dying. When I had Matty it took three days and I thought he was dead, I thought I was going to die and when I came home the colours were too bright I could only go out at night.

'Let me try and explain. You see you can't write about your own life exactly or it would just be like screaming so you change it about a bit and by the time you've finished and put all these people through these perfectly ghastly situations the problems have become theirs not yours.

'So then you're free to go through the whole process again, in fact you have to go on doing it because that's the only way you can forget what a mess you are yourself. I mean the critics have been terribly nice and they say how clever she is, creating this real world, contemporary problems, all that. But it's not a world at all, it's a bolt-hole.

'If I were honest I'd write a scream but I daren't. The truth is I don't care who else is mad or crippled so long as it's not me and I don't have to look. Writing isn't looking it's running away.'

Drink, he had said, smoke, so she drinks and smokes. The camera is interested. It explores politely the implications of bottle and glass. Janet Craig-Cooper does not approve of Janet Johnson. Janet Johnson is tight and she may be a bitch.

'My husband? Is an angel who doesn't know I've killed him, the walking dead. He's someone in a story I made up and I can't live without him. I was dead and he came with me.'

There was an electricity cut so they did not see the programme, which was a pity since it made good telly and sold a lot of books. They read aloud by candlelight and held hands, because they were deeply in love, so far as love is possible. And they lived together after that for a long time, until they were dead.

Jennifer Dawson

The Adventuress

'Stack-a-byes', the Novice-Mistress pointed to the stack of folding beds in the corner of the bare, chalky classroom. 'But we don't unfold them till we go to bed at ten.' She ran her hand down their chipped metal frames: 'I think you'll find them quite comfortable. *We* do.'

It was a small room with a trestle-table down the middle and a blackboard against the wall. The Novice-Mistress stood there tall and smiling at the plywood door: 'I'm going to go through your things now, while you get changed. Then I'll tell you what I am removing, and you can sign for them.'

I put on the black cord suit, the stockings and white blouse. Then the Postulant's stiff white cap. It had a long white handle that hung down the back and creaked when I moved. The Novice-Mistress held out hair-clips in her thick grey pumice hands, and pierced its starch. 'Hair-clips,' she smiled. 'And tape. For you to make name-tapes.' She was still smiling.

My image of the new life wasn't shaken by the room or by her, or by the cap and the stacked camp-beds, or the yards of linen tape that had been unwound for me. I went down to the Chapel and prayed:

'I will go unto the altar of my God' – I was a Postulant – 'Even unto the God of my joy and my youth.' I was young and my cup was full. The ugly room; the ugly clothes; the bowls of steaming milk-pudding and jugs of hot water; the ugly community house like a telephone-exchange beside the railway-track.... No, my cup was full and ran over.

For three weeks. Until the other Postulant came back from a farewell visit to the world.

I was standing there with my copy of St Augustine's *City of God*, which had been allowed me from my possessions, when she bounced in.

'Oh, you lucky thing!' she exclaimed at the book in her crisp, educated voice. 'You've discovered the *De Civitate*!' She pronounced it 'Dee Syeveetatey', and when I looked rather puzzled, she explained that this was Oxford's way – where she had been put to book.

'The *De Civitate*! How I do envy you. How I should adore to have *that* moment again. And you've still got Grullen and Von Hügel to discover, you lucky *oiseau*. He's a poppet. A great friend of mine. But I'm on stronger meat now. And so it goes on,' she sighed. 'There's no do-it-yourself kit where Christ is concerned. Unfortunately. Or fortunately' she smiled.

Her complexion was very clear; her cheeks flushed and excited. She was looking at me. I looked back into her large protuberant eyes. They were grey and very beautiful, and she made darting but graceful movements round the room as she spoke. 'I'm just battling with St Basil. I don't know whether you are like me and always get the Basils mixed up and confused, poor darlings.'

I didn't get them confused. I had never heard of them till that moment. My conversion had been from the real world. I had spent ten years sub-editing in a small London publisher's. Ten years shifting words across pages and back again – little black words like nuts and bolts, screwing them together and unscrewing them, laying them in rows and chains along the white page, tinkering with the row, obliterating it, and gradually coming to love only those things that could not go into words – the unspeakable that could never be caught in that mechanic's chain. And then, one day, I encountered it:

'The thing that is not love or hate or pity or scorn, but

the very breath of life, fierce and coming from far away.'
It was Bertrand Russell's God that I encountered, and lived
in the happiness of a spring evening for over a year as
though I had been caressed.

It joined and bound everything I saw and heard, and
when I read George Herbert's:

> Can there be any day but this?
> Though many suns to shine endeavour.
> We count three hundred but we miss.
> There is but one and that one ever . . .

I applied to be admitted to the Convent of the Holy Heart.
But I had never heard of the St Georges or the St Basils, or
the schematized life.

'Of course,' the Novice-Mistress had assessed me doubt-
fully at the interview, 'you may find that you aren't on the
right wavelength here. You may find that you want to get
married', she gave a slight sudden laugh, 'and raise a family.
After all' she added, standing up to end the interview.

'I've never thought of myself as cut out for that,' I had
replied censoriously thinking of the other girls in the office:

'What does he do, your brother?'

'He's at Oxford.'

'Lucky you having a brother at Oxford. I'm jealous.'

'No, you needn't be. He's a recluse.'

'Bad luck. Still, if you played your cards well. . . .' I des-
pised the managed life.

'Well, we'll have to see.' The Novice-Mistress showed me
to the door. 'The testing-time' she murmured half to herself, tapping her collar-bone.

The testing-time began when Sister Cuthbert, the other
Postulant, took me in hand and stared into my face with
her enormous grey eyes:

The Jameses and the Basils. 'Then there's that other
threesome that beginners often confuse, namely the three
St Georges.'

'I can only think of one', I scratched under my Postulant's cap, 'the one who slew the dragon.'

'Ah yes,' she nodded. 'Cappadocia. Yes.' She tapped her fingers on her forehead. 'Yes. The dragon of sin, or perhaps, more precisely, the Probi, that nasty messy heresy that tried to slew the church into –' she looked away. 'Have you come across that heresy yet? Pretty rum stuff. I'm grappling with St G. of Cappadocia for my special devotions. I did think of St Wilfred of Rheims. He's a real darling, a real poppet of a saint, and he would hear all my prayers I'm sure. Even when I'm feeling rather silly and female. Most women adore him. Father Boyle says the reason why women adore him is their special emotional needs. I'll show you something that he has done for us recently. Quite recently. Only you must keep it dark.'

Sucking her teeth and her cheeks in with anticipation, Sister Cuthbert led me over the railway-tracks and up into the school playroom:

'We prayed *so* hard. We even missed Compline we were praying so hard, the children and I. We had a special intention as well, during the Holy Family. . . . Isn't it wonderful?'

She opened the door. The playroom was black and empty. At the far end, beside the window, stood a record-player with 'Warners of Brixton' written on the inside of the lid.

'Isn't it super? We don't know how it happened. We prayed for six months and then, well, the miracle just happened and here we are.'

It stood in the corner, small and squat and black. A streak of sunlight opened up the corner and shone on a spider's web. The light swayed and went. The record-player remained – small and hunched and defiant, like a lump of raw meat. I was slightly shaken. Just slightly.

Sister Cuthbert took a deep breath and let it out. She inhaled the atmosphere slowly. She at least was going to stick up for God in this peculiarly unresponsive century.

'I wish He would be as obliging about granting our requests *re* sin, and help us out of all our private scrapes as willingly and speedily as He gave us this.'

'Did He give it willingly and speedily?' I asked involuntarily. But Sister Cuthbert wasn't going to shy off this question of God's adverbial attributes.

'Six months' she cried in a loud voice. 'Only six months.' I had a stirring of uneasiness. And another when she dropped to the floor on her knees beside the record-player:

'I must pay Him my respects, here and now.'

(No, please don't!)

But she had begun in a high voice: 'Oh God, we do indeed thank Thee for Thy gifts.' I mentally kicked at the little stubby paws that held the record player off the ground while Sister Cuthbert went on in her high prayer voice.

It was not her normal one. Not her clear upper-class Oxford accent, but a shrill Protestant one with a slightly Welsh intonation and a slight trill:

'Oh Lord! as if Professor Freddie Ayer and all those other Oxford philosophers who make snide remarks about Thee and question the power of prayer. . . . I mean, Lord, for example, take *Language, Truth and Logic* . . .' Never having read this book, I couldn't follow the rest of the prayer. My eyes turned back to the intransigent 'Warners of Brixton'.

'Lord, remember Kant's great "as if" – Or was it Ernst Weichert's? – Oh Lord, remember William James and the Will to Believe. Oh Lord,' Sister Cuthbert's voice rose angrily, 'ignore the sceptics and the linguistic philosophers. They can't possibly upset the applecart.' Her eyes bulged as she prayed. I found myself christening her Henrietta, after Henry James's adventuress, Henrietta Stackpole.

A bell rang. The adventuress spoke in her normal voice again:

'Goodee! Tuesday! One of Sister May's gorgeous apple-dumpling dinners! I shall put on pounds! Oh, the flesh! What a glorious bore it is. I suppose that one day this envelope of muscle and bone and tissue which is always doing the dirty on me and playing me up – Incidentally, even on such a small issue as nerve and muscle and ribonucleic acid, the Church has got the sceptics one hundred per cent wrapped up!' Another bell went. She finished her guided tour of the human organism later.

During the next three months, I learned how to curtsey and obey. I learned plainsong and chant. I learned how to sew and clean. I studied Christian doctrine, and received instruction from Father Boyle. I mastered the Collects and Offices, and learned the night ones by heart. I worked hard, and throughout that period, Sister Cuthbert never left me. During the long spells of compulsory silence, she would give me one of her wide excited grins, and push her thumbs up to encourage me, or give me the victory salute to show me that 'someone was doing fine'.

And yet she never ceased to surprise me by her originality. She was totally unpredictable. On Sundays, we went to the Estates, and she would leave me to narrate the weekly Bible story to the fidgeting children, and hold up flannelographs of Mr and Mrs Mankind in their Father's House, while she mysteriously disappeared behind the multipurpose altar. It had many uses. They were explained to us. It could become a canteen and coffee bar on youth-club nights, and a vaulting horse for the young men who never came.

'And quite right too,' Sister Cuthbert agreed. She didn't hold with brainwashing and indoctrination of the young. She shrugged off this aspect of religion; rejected any responsibility for it: 'After all, if we are merely interested in making them into nice, well-behaved young citizens, then the psychiatrists can do it much better.'

So she would sit behind the reversible altar reading psychiatry till the Sunday school closed, sucking odd sweets that the children had left behind, arguing with the parish priest, or pocketing the collection pennies and sixpences that had been abandoned on chairs and ledges so that she could have a good feed from a slot-machine on the way home to the community, a couple of coloured sweets shooting out of it into her habit, along with a plastic duck or trumpet which she passed on to a child in a pram passing

Jennifer Dawson

by as she chewed; then for no reason that I could see, she would suddenly stop and stare at me:

'Is there something wrong?' She looked hard. The sugar ball bulged in the side of her mouth. She waited for me to lose my faith.

Every evening before Vespers, there was an hour's recreation, and the Postulants and Novices would sit together with the Novice-Mistress, Sister Adeline, in their sitting-room, sewing veils and wimples for their 'clothing', for their 'bottom drawer' as Sister Cuthbert impishly called it, sucking at an imaginary toffee or sweet ball on her teeth.

'Do you think it's going to rain, Sister?' a small pious, ghostly voice would start the conversational ball rolling gently down the slope of our Rule.

'Oh surely, because Father Boyle is taking his umbrella, and *that always* makes it rain!' a brave soul would reply.

Gentle play. Gentle laughter. Then Sister Cuthbert would enter:

'They say the reason why it is always raining at Oxford is because, in the Middle Ages, they wanted the students tamed –' The Novices loved to hear about Oxford.

'For Matriculation,' Cuthbert would explain, 'you all march with your Dean to the Sheldonian in caps and gowns, except for Christ Church where they are told as they assemble in the quad that: "Caps will not be worn".'

'Really? Is that so?' we marvelled.

'All except Christ Church,' Cuthbert repeated. 'It's one of the ancient rights and privileges of "The House" – as it is called – Their Fellows are never called "Fellows",' she explained. And she was away. Prayers for the souls of those who died at Agincourt. 'Stat.Pup.' Not wearing gloves with academic dress. 'And you must always say "New College". Never just "New",' she ended.

'New,' I shaped the word.

But the other Novices were smiling, seemed to be enjoying the glimpse: May Morning; punts on the river; St Frideswide's Day. They murmured softly about history and continuity and the stablising effect of tradition on a society. So Sister Cuthbert went on about Sconces, University Sermons, Bulldogs, being progged, and beer-and-buckle-shoes.

'And Cambridge.... That must be a very old and beautiful place too,' they ventured.

'Some day perhaps we might arrange a visit there for you all,' the Novice-Mistress intervened.

'Sister, that would be beautiful.'

'Beautiful' they stitched, directing their words as exactly as their needles, their feelings as carefully as though they were putting down eggs.

I panicked. I saw our needlework floating through orchards of fat apples. I saw the food-hall check-out of a big London shop, and felt suddenly nostalgic for the sweaty night smell of stale food. When I came round they were talking about the 'Dark Night of the Soul'.

'Or "dryness" as it is often called,' the Novice-Mistress was informing us in her cool pleasant professional tone.

'Or if you want the technical name,' Cuthbert added looking at me, ' "Aridity".'

'Yes, that's right. Aridity,' Sister Adeline conceded, but firmly, 'sometimes it can go on for years, and a spiritual adviser may suggest....'

'Oh please Sister, not St Antony!' Cuthbert came back at her, 'the first time I tried St Antony, I found I had knocked up the wrong one. I'd got hold of St A of Padua – the one who finds all the things you've lost – instead. I was at school then, and dear me! For a whole month I couldn't lose all the things I always wanted to lose.' Someone gave a small click with their throat. The rest of us waited silently spellbound as she went on: 'I desperately wanted to lose my wretched homework and hockeystick, but St Antony must have worked overtime keeping our beastly homework safe. So you see, not Padua please, Sister, unless you want to let loose a thousand devils in this Novitiate.'

There was a pause at the end of the joke. They supposed it was a joke. A small plump Novice of about fifty put her hand to her mouth and I watched her wind rise slowly from her belly, through her chest to her mouth. But she fought it back and there was silence.

'Yes, aridity,' Sister Adeline repeated, as though Cuthbert hadn't spoken. 'Of course a lot of it is caused by sin and pride.'

'Technically known as *hubris*,' Cuthbert capped her. The middle-aged Novice put her hand to her mouth again. There was another silence. Then Cuthbert looked at the Novice-Mistress: 'Incidentally, wasn't it you I was having the argument about the *Corpus Juris Gaetano* with?'

'I suggest that you get some work out of the cupboard, Sister Cuthbert.'

In the corner stood a yellow plywood cupboard on wobbly legs. In it were kept toy animals with silly grins and drooling mouths; knitted rabbits that hung from our needles at recreation like defective babes; bits of embroidery with half-depicted scenes from the lives of Saxon saints who turned clothes into goats and jewels into pebbles; and mock-ups of the convent as it was planned and never built a hundred years ago.

Sister Cuthbert stared at the shelves full of soft toys, shell-necklaces, knitted dishcloths and illuminated prayers. She bit her lip. She clutched my sleeve:

'My dear! What a wizened array! What would I have to say for myself if the Lord confronted me while I was standing at this cupboard? Have they never heard that Beauty is Truth? Have they never heard of Ruskin and Walter Pater? No, they won't get *me* to make these diseased offspring, or to sell them. Who do they think we are? "The Old Timbers Tea Rooms"?' But the Novice-Mistress was towering over us with her loaded tray of souvenir articles, smiling and inviting us:

'What would you like to make, Sister Peter-Mary? And you, Sister?'

So Sister Cuthbert remembered her vows of Poverty and Obedience and Labour, and took a blind, drooling rabbit by the ears and started slowly to seed it with teeth and eyes, murmuring grimly to herself and to me that had a similar situation arisen in the seventh century before the Synod of Whitby, the Bishop himself couldn't have dragged her to that servile, shameful, female cupboard:

'If that's what Poverty and Obedience mean, I should have joined the Canvas Cathedral section of the Church. Why even Henry VIII – even good old Hen. 8 – in his dispute with the Abbess of Rosney didn't dare to put that one across about the position of women. Do you think Sister Adeline realizes that the whole question of the individual Religious and her autonomy was settled quite satisfactorily thank you, during the Northumbrian Renaissance. It was all over before Will. Conq. had ever been heard of on these shores.' But she was interrupted just then. A calendar was being passed round for us to admire. It was a picture of a mouse and a cat peering at each other through the bars of a chair. 'Peekabo' it was called. It had been presented to us by one of the Community's regular retreatants. We passed it round politely, smiled and exclaimed dutifully:

'The poppets.'

Then it reached Sister Cuthbert: 'I'm going to transfer it in appliqué-work onto the sleeves and back of my habit,' she whispered to me. Her thumbs rose above the top of the table. 'Resist!'

'Resist' I smiled back.

'As I said,' she wrapped the ears of her rabbit round a bundle of rosaries, then the bell went for the end of recreation, 'as I said, that was all sorted out, bar the shouting, before William the Conqueror.' She put her finger to her mouth. 'Hey! Do you want to see something?' She led me to a window that looked over a yard where the convent washing hung out – ten pairs of raw yellow wool combinations – 'Somebody's passion-killers aren't quite as white as they should be,' she sang. I laughed. 'Somebody's grouse-shooters have been slit up the crotch. Vandalism!' I laughed again.

'I don't think I shall last for very long here!' That was a great mistake, that remark. Sister Cuthbert paused and stood very still, looking at me with her big grey protuberant eyes. 'God eludes me here,' I said. 'I'm still in the world of words and things.'

She stared; her eyes went through the piles of plastic travelling altars and handy-bags; her eyes passed over the ten pairs of coms. I had made a grave error, so she was busy relating material substance to spiritual for me, time to eternity. She was outlining Kant's framework of perception: 'Even Bertie Russell hasn't got round that one' she raced backwards through history till she reached the Heraclitean fire. My mind went to a book I had seen pushed inside her folding bed: *Peak's Guide to the World's Great Thoughts and Their Thinkers.*

'You see, once you start doubting, you've got to go the whole hog, and question everything, not just God, but tables and chairs and even these lovely daffs,' she straightened a vase of daffodils, 'that we are all revelling in at the moment.'

I moved away so she repeated it, firmly straightening the daffodils again, watching my doubt, and coming after me: 'These lovely daffs that we are revelling in at the moment. Aren't we? Aren't we? Just say yes, and all the sceptics and scientists and materialists and linguistic philosophers will drop into our laps like ripe plums. They couldn't hold out an instant against these lovely daffs. Of course,' she conceded, 'there *is* the space–time Proof.' She drew out a pencil and paper and began a diagram. 'As well. Is *that* what was worrying you? The *episteme* business? Be careful! I must be careful, or I may find myself with a heresy-and-a-half on my hands. No, of course. Of course you don't. The real mystery is about the ordinary simple beautiful things round us like these daffs. . . .' As her hand went out to straighten them in their pot again, my vocation went. She seemed somehow to be hitting them.

That night at tea, the Sisters all seemed very old. The Order was dying. In the Community proper, there were only ten of them left. Ten in a refectory built for five hundred. Ten shuffling slowly forwards at Festivals, their worn black habits flying up like ragged chewed fur. Sister Marina swinging the censer shakily among the birds; Sister Anna chanting thinly behind; and the red-haired Sister — Red-Head, though she had no hair to see, only a fierce white angry face behind the Cross she was carrying — I saw her riding out hunting angrily between the dusty convent bushes for dogs and mice and children, then catching them in her white hands and crushing them, then peering again with red eyes into the box and laurel, huntress with a red dog, hunter of hated convent children.

The white linen flying through orchards of fat apples. The red-headed huntress with her dog. Other thoughts of greater irreverence and irrelevance came to me when I should have been at work or prayer. They came compulsively, obsessively, uncontrollably. As some people have to count up to ten each time a car passes, and others have to get to the steps in threes, and others must not tread on the black, so these thoughts slipped the bark of my brain, and reappeared again and again, self-generating, uncaused, gratuitous, unappeasable, unopposable, belonging nowhere, least of all in the brain from which they streamed:

'How many ounces of air come out of the mouth per prayer? Per word? Per syllable?' I would ask myself. 'And do they come out horizontally or vertically? End-to-end, or side-by-side? Longitudinally or latitudinally?' the questions persisted as the prayers went on. Sister Cuthbert watched my condition with sympathy, and drew out her pencil and paper or the back of an old discarded Holy Picture for diagrams and proofs. The Reverend Mother watched me calmly when I told her I had lost my faith.

'Yes,' she said. She was a small, carved, neat woman, and gave an inscrutable Chinese smile inside her stiff glass bonnet: 'Certainty is given only to a very blessed and saintly few. Did you think,' she puckered her face into a smile and I saw that she was very, very old, 'did you think that God would hand Himself out as though his Holy Spirit were like those free gifts they apparently give away in the shops these days?' Her voice was small and high and aristocratic. She offered me a newspaper, several days old: 'There is an article on the Essenes that might interest you. Keep it as long as you like.' She leaned forward and stroked my wrist with her pencil: 'I shall be praying for you.'

'Yes, but I'm wondering whether I'm cut out for this kind of life.'

'We are wondering too. We are all wondering. We'll see. Won't we?' she rose and held the door for me, keeping up the loyal pretence of 'We' in the large empty cloister.

The bathchairs were stacked at the far end. The aged Sisters sat imprisoned in the Infirmary above, because there was no one to push them out but Sister Cuthbert and myself. We tried to rope in other members of the Novitiate, but one said she had a bad back, and another always hissed 'Number Eight' at us, which was the number written on the door of the room from which medicines were nightly dispensed. Cuthbert and I would give each bathchair two quick runs up as far as the sweet-shop and back. When we had got through them all and returned breathlessly to recreation, the conversation would be making its usual headway:

'The weather looks as though it may hold out for a short walk.'

'Just a short one, perhaps.'

'Oh no, Sister, because Father Boyle is taking his umbrella, and that is sure to make it rain.' There was the usual titter of the suppressed life. Words lagged. Then the bell went for tea and there was a cry of dismayed relief:

'Already? Oh dear! How quickly the time flies, Sister. Too bad.'

Sister Adeline, the Novice-Mistress, looked at me.

'We were wondering,' she said. 'There's an exhibition on. Florentine Books of Hours, and the Roumanian Art Treasures. Is there anything else you would like to see ... while you make up your mind?' She smiled kindly at me, and sympathetically; only I wasn't allowed to go alone. Sister Cuthbert had to accompany me. Even among works of art, I couldn't escape her care any more than the Saints and God himself could. She would eye me solicitously as we made our way to the bus-stop:

'How goes? How does? How is the Fellow with the Scaly Tail these days?' And as we walked down the galleries she would launch into an account of The Devil through the ages, or the structure of the photon, or the wall of the nucleus, or the Archbishop of Paris's struggle with the Abbess of some small provincial order, with riders on the authority of men, the structure of the mid-brain, the cortex of mammals, moral factors in endocrinology, or the importance of the duck-bill platypus to Christian evolution, disengaging herself now and again from these themes to nudge me reproachfully because I had missed a glorious bit of detail on the Rubens Madonna's sleeve-band:

'Try not to miss things like that', and while she was still indignantly drawing my attention to the edge of the sleeve-band, she was drawing my own arm against hers to explain that 'what the Theological Indifferentists were trying to affirm was surely on the right lines as far as sin and all that mess and misery of shop-soiled trash was concerned. . . . Don't miss that darling little poppet of a minor Etruscan saint in the bottom left hand corner.' On the bus going back to the community, she would continue her analysis while the other passengers stared. 'You see, if you believe one-hundred-per-cent in the devil and all his works. . . . If you are in favour of showing up sin in all its pokiness – Yes, sin is like a run-down shop with all its shutters up, waiting for demolition – ' as silence fell in the bus, her voice rose, 'slum-clearance. Oh God, we do thank Thee for slum-clearance' I could hear the Protestant colliatura beginning in her throat, 'Oh God, we do of course, believe in slum-clearance, but Oh, God, what is the point of physical slum-clearance and all your nice brand new estates, when the mental feed-back remains, Oh God?' The bus sat spell-bound. The conductor gave free rides all round. The driver drew back the little window he was forbidden to touch. 'Of course, a lot of modern slum-clearance programmes are just licensed greed. And sex too. Sex has got to be taken into consideration by any wise person who doesn't want to throw the baby out with the bathwater. Oh Lord,' Cuthbert ended. 'Sister Peter-Mary, this is our stop.'

We got off. Thirty faces watched us from the bus. 'The Pilgrims to Walsingham were older, wiser people. Ban-the-Bombers are all very well, but oh, Walsingham, you were wiser.' She looked at me, but there was no reply, so she stuck her thumbs up: 'I'm praying for you. Oodles and oodles of prayer.' She almost winked. I grew more and more depressed.

Christmas came, and we decorated the house with fir and holly, and tied little bags of raisins in secret places for hide-and-seek, and set up stalls on Christmas afternoon in the refectory to sell each other embroidered handkerchiefs the infirm Sisters had made, bedsocks, and coconut-ice.

Christmas passed and the winter came. Rain slipped daily out of a white mist that hung over the streets like fine hair and meshed the windows and walls in its soft white net fur. Damp rose in the bricks. Wet rose up from everything. I took to leaving my under-clothes on all night so that they wouldn't be too damp in the morning. Spring would come, I told myself, but instead, the winter plugged itself in more tightly, and lay there gripping the roads in semi-dormant ice – black, half-submerged patches clamped in the yards where the sun never reached. In my fantasies, a man with a horn climbed over into the yards and unlocked them with his breath and sailed them away like kites. The thaw.

'But even if the spring does come,' I repeated to myself, peering out under the slanting iron vent of the bathroom-window, 'what?'

The snow was tweedy-speckled with grit; root and stone bulged through black; bone and tin and hair-clip and ashes, a flattened shoe, and the long neck of a skinny cabbage rattling and shaking in the draught that whistled through the broken patches in the corrugated iron fence. In the room below, the Novices were at recreation, making toys for deprived children, and sewing at their 'clothing-day veils', while someone read animal poetry aloud. I went to the

Reverend Mother's room, but was told she was away.
There was silence in the Novices-room when I went in.
Then Sister Cuthbert sprang up from her work:

'Oh please, everyone! All! Can you all do a Novena tonight for a cousin of mine who is itching to marry a Turk?
We don't approve of the family. At all. Our family doesn't.
The match would be disastrous. So I'd be grateful if you
could all do a Novena so that he would be spirited away,
this Turk, and fall in love with some lovely oriental girl.
Preferably Muslim, but definitely not Catholic.'

Until this moment, Cuthbert had occasionally seemed
like an ally. Now she seemed the most destructive and vulgar
woman I had ever met. The Novices sat very still when she
had finished her specifications. At last Sister Adeline said
coldly:

'You would do better, Sister, to keep your prayers for
Sister Thomas who has been in the Infirmary for so long
now. Or you might pray for the peace of the world.'

As usual, Cuthbert was temporarily subdued. She made
no attempt to contrast the Novice Mistress's thoughts un-
favourably with the Thoughts of Mao tse-Tung. She made
no whispered allusions to the Revisionists within the
Church, or selling the pass. She bent over her work for a
long time in silence. When I looked at her again, her eyes
were shut, and she was deep in prayer. Her penitence was as
managed and deliberate as her mischievousness, though.
This was the way God liked his soldiers, her large closed
eyelids seemed to say; high-spirited, bloody-minded sometimes, not unfamiliar with the Fellow with the Scaly Tail,
but at heart: 'Personally, I dig Him'. Her eyelids were open
again and she was smiling. 'And I dig good firm strong
Sister Adeline who knows how to cope with us all; in short,
I dig the whole set-up. Next time I get unstuck, you must all
rally round and heave poor old Humpty-Dumpty back on
to the wall again with lashings and lashings of prayer.'

I was completely numb and crushed when snow fell
again. This time it got melted by the smokey air and never
reached the ash-paths of the convent yard or our corrugated

iron walls and roofs. But the ice dug its teeth in, then snow fell yet again and stayed. I felt and saw and tasted nothing except its dead grey felt. Sister Cuthbert examined my condition carefully:

'Is there anything we lot can do about this thing?' she scratched her head, 'apart from a terrific amount of prayer. And of course, the gift and great grace of Confession to get really clean and stoked up before the really grisly part begins.' She was very close to me by the end of this prescription. I stepped back, but she followed me. I went downstairs and stood in the little graveyard by the railway track, looking at the bare tombs and the wooden crosses blackened and defiled by boys. 'Of your charity, pray for the soul of Sister Peter-Mary, died in the fifty-seventh year of her profession.' We lived long, didn't we, something in me cried as I stared at the squat black crosses like mushrooms sprouting on a bed of rubble and brick. I began to over-eat. I would stay behind in the refectory after the other Sisters had passed into the chapel for the Office, and stuff stale toast and heels of cheese and unconsecrated Host wafers into the deep pockets of my habit. 'The eyes of all them do wait upon Thee' I would hear the chant begin as I heaped spoonsfull of sugar into my mouth. My throat hurt with the sweetness, and a trail of sugar stuck round my mouth and on my hands and grew black with the soot it seemed to suck from the dirty streets around. The snow began to shift a little, to shuffle on the roofs and slide towards the gutters. I could smell the stiff tufts of grass thawing along the stony railway tracks. Spring was coming. In a week the Reverend Mother would be back and I would be gone. Sister Cuthbert beamed with delight when she saw how my mood had changed. She had fought for this so hard. This thaw.

They had all been to Confession and come back with a look on their faces that always frightened me and put me off that particular Sacrament. There was one man in the convent, and that was Father Boyle. Every week, they laid themselves open for him.

There was a suppressed excitement in the atmosphere

before they went in to him. When they came out, their faces were flushed and yet calm. Sister Cuthbert's eyes seemed to protrude more than ever when she exclaimed:

'How wonderful to have all that sheer grime washed away for another week.' She scrutinized me hawklike. 'I don't know *how* it works. But work it does. And with a vengeance. As I know only too well. And to my cost. But what a super thing grace is. Such a clean feeling.' I smiled. In a week I would have my money and clothes back and be gone. I smiled again. They saw my smile. The thaw they had worked for so long and so hard had indeed come. They smiled back.

'We knew he would. Bless him. St Jerome. I knew he would get you back. And so speedily and swiftly.'

'Did he do it speedily and swiftly?'

Cuthbert scratched the top of her nose and calculated. 'The next time, it will be easier. Like having a baby.' The bell went for tea. 'I'm starving. I'm eating like a wolf', she tucked in. Soft strings of cheese swung from her teeth. 'You see, for the last four days we've been fasting for you. Praying and fasting like mad. But now the thaw has come and we can all tuck in.' She helped them all to more while she outlined the history of Christian feasting. Then in a mellow, after-confession mood, they started to play 'The Flower Game'.

'Sister Adeline is a sunflower' someone bowled off gently, 'because she is so tall and stately.'

'And so near to the sun.'

'And Sister Teresa is an orchid. So rare and yet so tender.'

'And Sister Peter-Mary', they looked at me, 'is a big pink English rose. A tender old-fashioned cottage rose.' Unfortunately, just then a floral cardboard box was brought to table. 'What is it? A parcel? Who for? Whose birthday is it?'

'I found it inside Sister Peter-Mary's stacka-bed when I was dusting,' Cuthbert said with great simplicity. It was the box where I kept my secret stores of food. I would take it to the bathroom in the off-hours and eat.

Jennifer Dawson

'Open it, Sister. We are dying to see what it is.' Inside lay three slices of bread, a piece of mutton with someone's denture marks still in – before they had thought better and withdrawn from it – a slice of cake, and about thirty un-consecrated communion wafers. They all gazed and began in their traditional way to exclaim:

'How beautiful!' Then they stopped and stared at the *trouvaille*, and turned it this way and that to try and in-terpret it: 'This way up. No, the other.' I slipped out of the room, but Cuthbert followed me. I could hear her squeak-ing leather shoes on the other side of the bathroom-door when I had locked myself in. She was describing the scrub-up, the turn-out she had just had. 'Sister Peter-Mary, Confession, it is super-duper once so much mess and misery has been written off. You'll feel so good and clean again.' I buried my face in the dusty, fume-drenched curtains. I smelt the smell of London in summer. I heard the voices of men, and the sounds of taxis going round and round, and mothers' voices calling into the streets for their children. I could hear Cuthbert's leather shoes still squeaking outside the door. I put my head out of the window. I could hear the click of the garden Sister's spade in the hard acid ground, touching stone, hitting it again and again with a clear ring-ing sound. Metal against flint and soil. Penetration. I hit Cuthbert on the face when I unlocked the bathroom-door and saw her still standing there outside with her expression set to understand even that:

'*That* the Church has always been very very wise about', she tried to reconcile me with my desire. 'Except perhaps the Neriani who've always, let's face it, been as hard on other people as they are on themselves, probably because in the tenth cent— ' But I was running as hard as my narrow wool skirt and starched bonnet would let me. She was running after me.

'Look!' she was crying, 'having got so far, it would be a great pity to let the Fellow – ' her face was red where I had struck her. The piece of paper on which I had started to list my sins blew out of my hands and into the dirty hedge.

'Look! My sins have blown away.' She eyed the paper as it twisted into the street together with a paper bag stamped 'Happy Mothers' Day to All Our Customers'. 'My sins have blown away' I repeated.

'Indeed they have. And I can explain why', Cuthbert pulled a battered holy picture of the Madonna being assumed into Heaven from her pocket and bent it over so that only the printer's name was visible, 'because I have got PROOF.'

'I don't need proof,' I smiled. The air was suddenly warm and balmy. The wind came from the west and smelt of pines and lakes. But Cuthbert had broken back a bit of the hedge and made herself a little seat where she crouched and drew a diagram of her proof: 'Let me put it like this.' There was a long line which was God, and a circle which was the world, and the Incarnation joined them. She knelt down and joined them. She didn't seem to see that it was only *she* who was joining them and tying up God's love to his Creation. 'You see?' she cried triumphantly waving the completed proof. 'You can tell it like it is, where God is concerned.' The structure rested on her knees for a moment, then it too blew away. I laughed and laughed, and for a moment she joined me, and we sat there in the privet hedge side by side making it squeak and shake with our laughter. But when I got up and went down the road into 'Luigi's One-Two Hey-Presto All-Night Box' she saw she had played her last card and her triumph ebbed. She stood at its window for a moment looking in, first confident, then hesitant, then sad. She pulled out another holy picture, started another proof on its back, then made a final thumbs-up gesture and was gone.

I walked alone along the streets. I couldn't think how it was that the air was so sweet, the grass so full and green, and the birds so loud. The blackbirds were so glossy they seemed to have flown there from velvet ponds, and to perch and sing in places where birds do not usually go – on metal rods and clamps and hatches and valves; on brick wastes bearded with cement. They darted among the chimneys like kingfishers, and brought with them a wind straight from water-meadows and hedges where rain had just fallen. There were flowers with big yellow faces growing in bundles on the tops of old tombs in the churchyard, and a big white bird had just built a nest of long twigs it was still twining and binding among their yellow. Other white birds swooped at young branches the trees dropped lovingly for them. Oh beautiful world.

For years afterwards, I thought I might meet Sister Cuthbert again. Perhaps she was married, or living with another woman of her own views, having finally and irrevocably got across the Community infra-structure on the subject of the time–space framework, the autonomy of women, or her Proof.

Or perhaps God would grow tired of her support. Or she would go mad. One thing however I could not imagine, and that was that she should lose her faith. Her faith was not the kind of thing that could be lost, any more than her skin could be. One cannot lose faith in the extensions of one's will. She could only up the ante.

But one day, not long ago, as I sat in my bed-sitter reading my parish paper, I noticed that our prayers were asked that week for Mother Cuthbert of the Holy Heart, Clerkenwell, who was sailing for Peru next week to preach the Gospel to the man-eating Auca.

'She must have fallen finally and irretrievably foul of the Novice-Mistress' I thought. But then it struck me that she probably *was* the Novice-Mistress; or the Reverend Mother. And I had been sitting here all the time. Ever since she had driven me out of my chosen place. My vision of the un-schematized ineffable had never come back, and I had sat ever since in my bed-sitter or in the poky little office of 'Wise Nicodemus', a small Christian quarterly I worked on, measuring words and fitting them into chains and rows while she was making her God. Everyone needs to make something. She had made Him, and had obviously done it well. I had never made anything.

I sat there with my parish magazine thinking of her

making her God; picturing her make her man-eating Auca. And she would do well among them, I knew. She would learn their language quickly and wear their clothes where she could, and adopt their ways and sympathize with their sexual habits and try to understand their nutritional ones, even if she could not get as far as participation. But even that I would not have put beyond her, provided she had got in the safeguards – criteria of death and rules to make sure the soul had really quit. I could see her there in the jungle clearing in her jeans and slip-slops with her copy of *Great Thoughts and Their Thinkers* strapped round her waist, and The Gospels tied on a long stick to keep the flies away – Sister Cuthbert, a real Beat of a Religious.

Paul Winstanley

Urquhart

With painstaking precision, working to a tolerance of the smallest fraction of a millimetre perceptible to the naked eye, and scrupulously guarding his eye in its nakedness from the embarrassment of conscience to which it would be exposed by being tacitly asked to pass over as if unnoticed any failure to conform to the high standard of accuracy imposed by it in the incorruptible integrity of its supervision, Urquhart tore his bus ticket down the middle.

He began by pinching the edge of the ticket securely between the thumb and forefinger of his right hand – the tip of the thumb and the outer side of the fleshy pad of the fingertip – aligning the edge of the thumbnail with a black line printed feint down the centre of the pinkish-orange ticket; he then took an identical grasp with his left thumb and forefinger in such a way that the two thumbnails were pressed firmly together. Now, by a controlled counter-rotation from the wrists, he started the tear, continuing it by drawing his hands steadily apart with constant meticulous adjustment of the tension placed on the right and left portions of the ticket. He could actually see the microscopic fibres of the paper parting, and could perceive the minutest tendency in the tear to deviate to either side, which he would rectify immediately by altering ever so slightly the angle and force of the pull exerted by one hand or the other. When the ticket was almost in halves he paused, leaving the two strips connected by an isthmus about two millimetres in width. So far, he had achieved an admirable exactitude.

While performing this bisection, Urquhart was giving close and anxious consideration to his own mental state. I am on edge. Yes, overwrought. This realization had come to him – the sudden culmination of a long unconscious process – as he stood in the bus queue waiting for this bus. Behind him in the queue were two youths, in working blue jeans and black leather jackets whitened in the creases with cement-dust, with curly sideburns and candystriped shirts – one striped green, one pink – larking about (as Urquhart now describes it to himself, prim with indignation) all over the public footway; imperilling with their indecent energy the mandarin fragility of morning Urquhart. The ironshod boots clattering in fearsome playfulness on the pavement. Urquhart twitching with nervousness in the proximity of them. They had thick wrists and hands, limy encrustations under broken fingernails. I am absurd. A curio: a plexus of refined but redundant sensibilities in a porcelain box. Urquhart, you delicate dodo, why are you not extinct?

Sylv was the topic: riddled gleefully with a crossfire of fleering allusions, a codified repartee, defamatory and titillating. Who is Sylvia? what is she? academicized Urquhart. A tart in the canteen. Jammy them, then. (Better.) They exchanged complimentary abuse and shoved each other about, unbothered by the tutting curmudgeonly queue ('They'll knock someone right over in a minute if they don't behave'), romping and justling and sure enough cannoning into Urquhart's disapproving back, catapulting him out into the gutter at the very moment that the bus drew in to the kerb.

'Do you mind?' Urquhart quivered, flustered and gangling, his breathing bronchial with his agitation; and one of the youths grinning up at his rachitic six foot four: 'Wha's a matter mate? Y'aren't unner t'fuckin bus yit, are yer?'

Now, sitting in the bus, bookended in his seat by a stolidly obese woman, Urquart soothes himself with reasonable ratiocinations. Why do I allow myself to be put out by the mere vitality of adolescents with industrial boots on?

Because I am a chronic case of ingrowing intellect? Because I envy their robustness, their insouciance, their insensitivity? – in fact, their stupidity. Triumph. But does my recognition that I envy them obviate the envy? Unhelpful. But *do* I envy them? Am I afraid of them? no I am not afraid of them. What is there to them that I should be afraid of?

Thus Urquhart to himself (commentaried alter-Urquhart to himself). Self-analysis, these attempts of yours at self-therapy, are futile, you realize? Accounting for one's own behaviour is one's own behaviour as much as the behaviour it accounts for, and is still to be accounted for.

An inspector sidled down the bus, chickening his neck to see the tickets which the passengers displayed for him. He said twice 'Tickets please' to Urquhart's unattending ear before Urquhart started and opened his fist, to exhibit ten impeccably equal shreds of pinkish-orange paper. Apologetically, Urquhart arranged them on his palm to show the mystical figures, while the inspector, anglepoised in the aisle, assumed a countenance of patient martyrdom. 'Nerves, that is,' he accusingly diagnosed, moving on. In fact in my case this particular act is not symptomatic, because I always have torn up my bus tickets. Nevertheless, it is true that at present I am rather tensed up. Very, actually.

The morning passed, however, uneventfully, narrated Urquhart (to a one-eyed doodle on his every other Monday clean white blotter) as he looked up at the paranoiac office clock which marked the time in convulsive jerks of its minute hand, sixty to the hour, and which now over-emphasized twelve fifty-nine. Urquhart waited for the climactic tic, and went for lunch. He went as usual to the Tudor Restaurant. He ordered liver and bacon, specifying no peas, and was looking for his place in *Vathek* (his book-marker had dropped out, but he remembered, fortunately, that he had written on it a reminder to himself to ask Mrs Stojsauljevir about the gas meter) when Mr Grindle came in. Grindle looked about for a table: Urquhart pored upon his book. Grindle notices Urquhart and looks away hastily;

Urquhart peeping up to see if he is safely unseen; Grindle glances to check that he is really unnoticed: their eyes meet and the situation is irreparable. Grindle advances; Urquhart lays down his book.

'May I?'

'Please do.'

And Grindle seats himself, correcting the alignment of his dessert fork.

'Are you becoming a Tudor regular, then, Mr Urquhart?'

'I usually lunch here, yes. But I've not noticed you in here before.' (Untrue.)

And so forth. Limp dance of moribund politenesses. Grindle rallies – an inspired gambit – 'What's the book?'

'*Vathek*.'

'Never heard of it, I'm afraid.'

Urquhart offered no enlightenment: he was anxious to, feeling to the full his churlishness in rejecting the ploy, but before the prospect of a literary anatomy for the benefit of Grindle he quailed and sat silent, in shameful taciturnity.

Crescent hiatus. Grindle, self-despising victim of compulsive politeness, perseveres: 'Settling down all right in the department now?'

'Quite well, I think, thank you.'

'You'll have been here, what? three months now?'

'Six.'

'Long as that? From Eastbourne you came to us, didn't you?'

'Bournemouth,' apologized Urquhart.

'Oh yes. Lovely place, I believe. And what decided you to come up here?'

'Oh, I don't know.' He gestured hopelessly, unable to think precisely what it was that, half a year ago, had decided him to come up here. Something must have. Grindle waited expectantly, his expression of courteous interest magnificently sustained for three quarters of a minute and barely beginning to sag by the time Urquhart, desperately rummaging among implausible memories of motives, at last came up with the perfect explanation: 'Just fancied a bit of a change, I suppose.'

'Ah!' assented Grindle, in sympathy, agreement, perfect understanding; and, ducking his head over the plate which the waitress at that moment placed in front of him, he celebrated their mutual feat of communication with a forkful of processed peas.

Back at work, Miss Moss, pendulous with lumps of amber, evasively redolent of armpit, brightly plonked a ponderous wad of record-cards on Urquhart's desk. And paused sociably. Urquhart picked up one of the cards and scrutinized it, engrossed himself to the conscientious eyebrows in its labyrinthine decimals.

'Another batch,' observed Miss Moss, hearteningly.

Urquhart wordlessly assented. Go away.

'Finding your feet here now?'

Again? 'Oh yes. Quite at home.'

'That's good. Have you relatives in town, Mr Urquhart?'

'Relatives? No, actually.' How sad.

'Oh dear. Never mind, I expect you've some friends round about?'

'I know a few people, yes.' Vague smile to convey an inexhaustible acquaintance.

'Well, that's something. Dreadful if you don't know anyone. I do think a social life of some sort is so important.' She contemplated him kindly for a moment: 'Good': and exit, junoesque and courageously thirty. Harrison, who has been watching from his desk, dips his nib in the red ink and wipes it on his blotter.

This is preposterous. I see it all! – I see what they are up to: they are *taking an interest in me*. For my own good. They are worried about me.

They have formed a committee to consider my case and decide on suitable courses of action. He needs drawing out of himself. Moss, Grindle, Harrison, Mrs Willis, Miss Carmichael – they'll all be in it. Miss Moss, perhaps, is even offering herself. O joy. Miss Moss's tweeded rump rolling by my side. 'Gwendoline, I . . .'

He's shy, you know.

Oh yes, shy.

Living alone like that, bad for you.

Self-absorbed. Talking to himself.

No social life.

No properly cooked breakfast.

You can grow eccentric very quickly, you know.

We ought to try and do something for him.

Yes, let's.

No – it's intolerable! they're closing in, their smiles, their how's it goings their clappings on the shoulder their enquiries about the local organizations they have recommended to me and would I care to come round to supper next Tuesday? and I have knitted you these nice warm bedsocks Mr Urquhart. Finally, an arm round my sob-shaken shoulders, an offered handkerchief – 'Blow' – 'There, there' – and they bear me off, broken and inane, slobbering gratitude, a complete success. We did it. Good old Urquhart! Good old Archie! One of us.

I am aware that I am exaggerating. It is of course absurd to resent so neurotically the well-intentioned advances of one's quotidian co-workers. All that is necessary is to meet them halfway, to be a little cooperative in the knitting of cosy woolly relationships; to open and close the mouth like a happy imbecile fish, emitting the bubbles expected of one, the appropriate little exhalations of carbon dioxide. Just go through the motions, that's all that's required. Placate them. A word to Grindle about my collection of cacti; an indiscreet hint to Mrs Willis about having to see someone home last night; mention to Miss Moss my studies of de Sade for an extramural Ph.D. (maybe not). Just a few sops to their cannibal altruism. Or be frank; hugely polite but frank. 'Thank you for your kindly meant concern, but...' But.

Maniacally whipping up his unrighteous resentment into a psychotic soufflé of indignation, Urquhart at this point sensed the imminent effervescence of a reprehensible inspiration. Not allowing himself time to premeditate, he jabbed his pen into the red ink: and wrote in large childish capitals diagonally from corner to corner across the top record-card MISS MOSS HAS <u>B.O.</u>

He sat back and contemplated this with profound satisfaction; corrected the outline of an S; clinically examined his reactions and found them to be a sense of relief, release, fulfilment and self-declaration; blotted the card; and slipped it into the middle of the pile.

Then, mentally and physically relaxed, he began to work. His mathematics laddered agilely up and down columns of figures, totalling and deducting, dividing and percentaging, the calculations clicking smoothly and automatically through his emancipated brain.

At twenty-five to five he went to find Miss Moss to borrow the ink eradicator. His feeling that he was proof against the complotted altruists beleaguering him remained, however, unimpaired. The serene assurance of an invulnerable identity strengthened in him through the afternoon, and as he left work, nodding fearlessly to Mrs Willis, he formulated it in words: I am a match for them. Urquhart impregnable.

He knew, though, that feelings of this kind never acquired concreteness until they were due to crumble; and therefore he made the most of it. He took the bus only as far as the war memorial, and walked through the park, surveying from his mental fortifications the people he encountered. He refused to deviate from his path for a bloated middle-aged man constitutionalling in a bowler hat. He smiled with paternal benevolence at a girl pushing a pram, and with avuncular condescension at a small boy lurching by on one roller skate. He scowled at an elderly woman attending with patient solicitude a corpulent curly-haired terrier which squatted fatly shitting in the middle of the path. There should be a monument somewhere representing the English beldame in this characteristic stance, this attitude of devotion almost doglike: a statue in bronze, larger than life, the right hand drawing the garment about the venerable breast, the left deflected in the classic manner downwards and a little outwards, its comely gesture graciously extended via the leash to the small defecating quadruped. Satiric Urquhart.

He still felt invincible when he arrived back at his room. But while preparing his supper he wounded himself with the tin opener. It slipped off the rim of his tin of spaghetti and stabbed him deeply in the left forefinger. The pain straightened him out with a jerk, and he banged his head on the sloping ceiling: a shutter of soft blackness eclipsed his senses, pierced through with little bright tridents of pain, and ridiculously he fell on the floor. He got up again immediately and recommenced the operation of opening the tin, but before he was halfway round he noticed that his finger was dribbling blood. He wrapped his handkerchief around it and picked up the tin opener for the third time. Then he thought 'Blood doesn't wash out', and unwound the handkerchief; as he did so, Mrs Stojsauljevir trod on the creaking board outside his door and her guttural voice nervously enquired: 'Mr Urquhart? Are you all right?'

'Yes, quite all right, thank you', Urquhart holding his finger out at arm's length and watching the blood drip to the floor, fat glistening asterisks on the linoleum like hot solder.

'There was a terrible percussion.'

'It's all right. I dropped my tambourine.'

There was a silence, then the creak and shuffle and slop of her retreat, back to the icon and the television. Urquhart pondered means of stopping the bleeding. Eventually he tore a long strip from the edge of the local newspaper for three weeks back (which he had bought in the hope that there might be a small davenport advertised for sale) and wound it round and round the finger. He then finished opening the tin, plopped the spaghetti into his omelette pan, lit a match and turned on the gas ring. It gave a tiny sigh: the gas had run out again.

Urquhart felt for a shilling for the meter. As it was his habit to keep his small change in his left-hand trousers pocket, and as on this occasion he wished to avoid putting his left hand in his pocket, for fear of deranging the newspaper wound round his finger, he twisted from the waist and angularly inserted his right hand, first transferring to his left the still burning match. As he concentrated on scooping up the coins, the newspaper bandage caught fire from the match. He flapped his hand frantically, making whirls of sparks; his clenched right hand caught in his pocket and then suddenly came out, scattering money. The newspaper detached itself from his finger, and floated, burning and bloodstained, into the butterdish. Urquhart said 'Damn'.

Eating his spaghetti, he went over this sequence of mishaps, and noted with concern that they had occasioned him no spontaneous amusement. That rather indicates that my sense of humour is failing. At a low ebb. Ordinarily I would have seen the funny side. Ludicrous Urquhart. Of course a blow on the head is a foul of a unique kind, a deliberate treachery on the part of inanimate matter, and it is natural, is it not, to feel aggrieved? Sickened. And a lump like a harpy's egg. Nevertheless, I ought to have been able to laugh at myself. A sure sign of nervous debility. Nittering solitary insanity creeping up on me.

Vathek for once provided no solace: Urquhart's imagination kept wandering off into mindscapes less and more fantastic. The room was oppressive; and when the wallpaper began to fidget he got up and went out.

For the very end of October it was extraordinarily hot and close, he banally remarked to himself. On the corner there was a pub, which he had never been in. He chose the public bar on egalitarian principles. The walls were pine-boarded to elbow level, the wood dark brown with sticky pew-varnish; above that they were ochre yellow, the same as the ceiling. Urquhart requested a half of bitter. Next to him at the counter bulged a vast man in a houndstooth greatcoat, who looked at him, turned his shoulder and spread along the bar, taking up an additional foot by a mere slackening of his posture. Urquhart moved along. On his other side was a small dehydrated plumber with a baggy sports jacket over a brown denim bib and brace. He sparrowed at Urquhart's half pint and at Urquhart and said abruptly 'That'll do you no good, son.' North-country accent of aggressive hospitality. 'Ere, ave a pint on me.' He nodded to the barman. Egalitarian Urquhart flustered and stammered. 'That's most kind of you, but, thank you very much but – ' The barman looked from one to the other and back again and went away. 'Thank you all the same, very much, but I'm just in for a quick one', propitiated Urquhart. The man shrugged without resentment, gurgled at his own pint, and relapsed into contemplation of the foam-friezes round the inside of the glass. Urquhart drank his beer quickly, nodded embarrassedly at the little man, who bared his teeth in acknowledgement, and left.

At the next pub he went into the lounge. Between the ochre of the ceiling and the dark brown panelling the walls were papered dark red; the paper had a surface simulating plush, with a pattern derived from victorian upholstery. There were glass-topped tables, but Urquhart could not see anywhere to sit down. Jovial well-to-do men competitively plied their women with moustached gallantries. The women, metallic and glistering, tinkled with pleasure. It took Urquhart a long time to win the attention of the smart barmaid, who, talking, not looking at him, squeezed his fingers briefly as she handed him his change. He stood hemmed in by well-dressed backs. Choice tobacco smoke made his eyes water. A guffawing man jostled him and spilt half his beer: said 'Sorry, old man', dabbed at Urquhart's trousers with a white handkerchief, 'Bloody sorry, old chap' and turned away again: '– so I said to him, well, old man, I don't know what *you* expect from your secretary' (laugh laugh) 'but speaking for myself...'

Urquhart stayed for a second beer, and left with a headache at closing time. He was making his way home when suddenly he thought 'I could go and see Keith.' He stopped, considered, and then began to walk in the opposite direction. Off the main road the streets were abnormally quiet. The few people he saw – coat and hat figures hurrying ahead of him – turned corners almost at once and vanished. Everyone has gone to bed. A population made up exclusively of ladies of respectable age lay with the lights out, toothglass of water on the bedside table and empty chamberpot modestly out of sight, tucked up in their quilts and counterpanes, eiderdown and candlewick, still as the soft pellets of dust and fluff in the far corner under the bed, in their draughtless bedrooms behind heavy closed curtains of heliotrope bombazine.

The house where Keith lived was in darkness, but the front door was open and the glass door inside the porch unlocked. Urquhart entered the dark hall and felt along the wall for the time-switch. He pushed in the fat bakelite button with his thumb and the light came on on the first landing. Keith had the third-floor flat. The stairs were steep and narrow; short flights with oddly shaped interim landings. Not that the house was ancient; but it had been converted into flats and the staircase squeezed to a contorted shaft. Turn left, and left, and left again, and left again. These stairs require faith: they might never lead to anywhere. The time-switch switched the light off soundlessly. Urquhart climbed the last flight of stairs, which led straight up to a two-foot-wide shelf in front of Keith's door. He felt along the wall for the bell, and hesitated with his finger on it.

He was always afraid waiting for doors to open. The momentary hiatus before recognition, the time it took for features to arrange themselves: invariably a confrontation of two strangers. Footsteps and the hinging open of the door, and the expected person standing there, hand on Yale knob – the predictability of it was irrelevant. Always it was an unforeseen figure projected flatly onto the whitelighted rectangle, a stuck subliminal dawning with split-second gradualness; a demand on the unready mind.

Keith opened the door, and said 'Oh. Hullo. Come in.'

'Hullo', said Urquhart. He followed Keith into his living room.

There was a girl there – a pallid blonde, wearing a

mustard-coloured dress which emphasized her small bust and wide hips. She looked at Urquhart, then at Keith with an expression which required that he should explain Urquhart rather than introduce him.

'This is Archie Urquhart', Keith said. 'Veronica.' Urquhart and the girl touched fingers. 'Archie was in my form at school', expanded Keith, adding for Urquhart: 'Veronica teaches in the girls' half'.

He tried to do better: 'Archie's been up here three or four months now, and this is only the second time he's made the supreme effort to visit me. And a fine time of night he chooses to do it . . . No, honestly, you know you're welcome any time.'

'Actually I was on the point of going,' the girl said. 'I hope you don't mind.'

'Oh,' said Urquhart, floundering. 'If I've come at the wrong time. I mean if I'm breaking up your evening or anything?'

'Not in the least', the girl assured him conclusively. Keith meekly fetched her coat. 'Goodnight', she said, going.

'That was a filthy look,' said Urquhart when Keith returned. (Or can I still be so direct with old Keith?)

'What?'

'She gave me.'

'I didn't see.'

'I didn't know you had a girlfriend up here.'

'Didn't you?'

'Did I bust in on something?'

'No. That's all right.'

'Well, I'm sorry if I did.'

They sat for a while without speaking. A table lamp made from a bottle, its imitation vellum shade decorated with whisky labels, gave out a tired light which left shadows in the corners of the room. Eventually Keith said: 'There's some coffee in the pot. I'll go and hot it up.' 'Don't bother', Urquhart said. Keith went out to the kitchenette. Urquhart picked up a record from the floor and looked at the sleeve.

Bolero. He put it down again. Keith came in with the coffee pot and two cups and saucers, went out again and returned with milk and sugar. He sat down and leaned forward to pour out the coffee.

'What do you think of me?' he asked. He kept his eyes on the cups, adding milk to the black coffee, watching it curl and mingle.

O no. Urquhart squirming, pinned.

'How do you mean, what do I think of you?' The question squatted between them and pulsated at him, bare and indecent.

'Well, as a person. I mean, do I seem all right to you? I mean – well, do I seem a normal sort of character? Like anyone else.'

'You seem all right to me. How's the teaching going?' Change the subject.

'Well, that's what I mean. The kids seem to find something odd about me – you know, sniggering and all that.' His eyes watering. 'You wouldn't know what I mean. But now Veronica seems to have caught on to it too. Started treating me as if I was a bit queer. I mean, not *queer*; but as if there was something funny about me.'

Urquhart cowering in his chair, his sympathy trying to back out, covering up. Of all the victims to pick on, why me? 'I shouldn't let it bother you.'

'I can't help it bothering me. It *does* bother me. Hell, how would *you* feel? I mean, if everybody you came in contact with treated you as if you were some sort of a, a, a comical oddity. As if there was a joke about you that they wouldn't tell you. Like words written on your back.'

He looked at Urquhart, his soft face wobbling, flushed with misery. What am I supposed to say?

Keith went on: 'It's not as if I'm hypersensitive. I wouldn't care a damn, really. Only Veronica starting as well is a bit much. I mean, I haven't got anybody much to kick around with up here. I don't make friends easily. Veronica was the only person I felt I had anything in common with.'

He bent his head over his cup, in fear of Urquhart's resentful pity.

Urquhart said 'Do you think you could' (but what *does* one say?) 'be imagining it?'

Friendship. Embarrassing one another to our greater mutual discomfort. 'Of course, it's rather difficult for me...'

Keith shrugged abjectly. 'I'm sorry.' He stirred his coffee.

Thinking *I*'m treating him queerly too. O, writhing hell. What about me? the commiserating victim.

Keith reached behind the settee and brought up a bottle. 'Like some hock?'

'Oh, the coffee'll do me, thanks a lot. I ought to be going, actually.' Keith fetched two glasses from the cupboard and poured. Urquhart resigned himself.

Going back to his room sometime after two, Urquhart submitted himself to a salutary admonition. Obviously the private woes of a somewhat peripheral acquaintance (they are all peripheral, however) cannot be permitted to aggravate your personal malaise. Words on whose back? Assuming indeed that I have one to be aggravated; which I refuse to admit until such time as the symptoms (which in any case are not deserving of reliance unless they positively force themselves on me, instead of being conjured forth by morbid introspection, from which I resolve henceforward to abstain) have cohered into a recognizable syndrome. Only I am certainly very tired. I think I am not thinking well.

The night seemed freakishly warm; and all his senses seemed swollen, their impressions dilated and menacing. Perhaps I am feverish. Why should I be? Get a grip.

He walked through square backstreets hermetically ceilinged with the slab of night. Green lampstalks sprout between the pavingstones, fruiting above into sticky yellow light, casting a phosphorescent pollen on ornate green-painted wrought iron leaves of foot-wide balconies, on doorknocker grotesques and front-gate fleurs-de-lis. The heavy blackness laid across the roofs lids in the mummified street; the houses lean inwards under its weight; the street-lights cellar plants pallidly suffocating in subterranean warmth – anaemic shoots dead alive in a lifeless humidity of underground. No breathing in the street, and the dead air absorbs your footfalls.

Urquhart took the footbridge across the railway, hearing his feet clop woodenly on the plank steps. Below him a scimitar-curve of lines sheathing themselves curtly into the darkness. Descending on the other side he turned the corner in the steps and there was a body dumped against the wall.

Nothing. Then the downward steps behind him tilting him into his fright. Knees drawn up and shoes together but the trunk slumped sidelong and bald head toppled forward, bone white cobweb-fringed with grey. One hand palm upwards from a limp macintosh sleeve.

Urquhart watched the hand. Slowly he moved down the remaining steps: ten steps, ten pauses. He stood beside the body. The fingers of this hand curl in; flesh of the palm dear for nailing. One blow to drive it through – twenty to jar it into the adze-hewn wood.

But surely (surely not) the sleeve is empty. Above this threadbare cuff and bloodless wrist, nothing?

Urquhart placed the toe of his shoe alongside the hand and suddenly switched it sideways. He expected that the hoaxing hand with its stump of severed wrist would flip across the pavement.

The arm jerked with limp violence, helplessly, the knuckles flapping down on the gritty pavingstones. Shoulder dropping forward and the body collapses further on its side, head tipped mouth open on unjointed neck; knees and shoes though still together – straw-stuffing stiffened, a sackcloth effigy.

But time resumes. Urquhart bent nearer. Beerbile smell; and now a wheezing rise and fall of the breast under the cold sweat stuck shirt. Shallow scraping breaths of dead drunk. A spittle of stale vomit on the chin.

Turning away, and the closed eyes of the drunk man follow me hastening to the corner and after. If as I stood there heartbeatless, placing my foot to spurn, the eyes had opened; and if the impossible hand viperstruck to my ankle – claycold – and a rattling laugh.

Urquhart fantastical. Macabre Urquhart. (But his ear to his own self-satire deadened. Alter-Urquhart impotent.)

Hearing his muffled footsteps follow him, Urquhart walks through the streets between the sightless housefronts. Impenetrable houses wall in my going onward. They have no into. Stone opaque false windowframes and doorways giving on no rooms: cavewall carvings in solid schist and limestone in a tunnel to where? No opening off. Doors with no other side panel my passage down, my cannot otherwise, my must. The way is lit. Fluted and tendrilled lampstandards support their haloed pods on bracts and calyces. The lamplight glistens oilily against the soft earthwarm darkness, highlights on soot.

Fibrillated roots grow down through the mouldering black plush of the lid. Invisibly festooned, the air obstructs my nostrils. My bones are dry: brittle in the sockets. The houses crush in closer – kinaesthetic panic – the heavy blackness of the night bearing down on the roofridges. Ponderous soft caving in. Obliterating.

Urquhart.

I have an unhealthily fecund imagination, which must be checked. I am only tired.

He reached the corner and turned left. Two streets to go. In an upstairs window of one of the houses a light came on, behind primrose chintz bedroom-patterned curtains, and went off again; and Urquhart felt as if he had been spoken to, as if someone talking in her sleep (or in his sleep) had mumbled his name. He went on, making no reply; noting only that now he felt chilly. The road went uphill.

Perhaps I have flu. Mrs Willis says there's a lot going about. His breathing tasted coldly of pennies.

It occurred to him that he could take his temperature when he got in. Or could have if it hadn't been so late. Or early: since it must now be about two thirty. If it hadn't been so early?

Mrs Stojsauljevir being now certainly in bed and asleep; or in whatever state she entered into when she went to bed. If it had been earlier he could have asked her whether she by any chance happened to have such a thing as a thermometer which he could borrow, and if she had he could have taken his temperature, which might have supplied him with a reason for not going in to the office tomorrow (or rather today) – if there was any point in not going in to the office; which, since there was no point in staying in his room either, nor for that matter in doing anything else he knew of, there wasn't.

Jean Stubbs

Call me again the
Day that is Past!

In the early hours of a Wednesday morning Mrs Mannering encountered the fourth horseman of the Apocalypse. A finger tapped her lightly, firmly on the shoulder. A voice said intimately, clearly in her ear:

'What is the name of this horse?'

From a Methodist background she drew her answer.

'The pale horse.' Adding, 'and his rider is death.'

She woke to the shadows in her room, knowing the presence had gone. She switched on the bedside lamp and put a dressing gown about her shoulders. The mind, she thought, played strange tricks. But behind the conundrum of a dream lay reason, comforting as friendship. Why, that evening she had watched a film about horse-racing on the television. Only last month a former beau of hers had died. Mind wove such disparate straws into fearful fancy. And as one grew older, she understood, unpleasant dreams were the hazard of having too much past and hardly any future. This was in the nature of things. In the nature of them.

A pot of tea would be a delight, but she feared to face the dark well of the stairs, to brave the unlit house. She reached for a book, and read only the wrong lines, the images of sorrow and decay.

'I am afraid,' she said out loud, into vacancy, into the tumultuous ticking of the clock.

Tomorrow she would go to Donald Parker, family doctor, for a medical check. Perhaps some inward enemy sharpened his sword. Perhaps this was a warning from her kidneys, her liver, her bloodstream. Perhaps, living alone, she brooded and should take more exercise of mind and body. Perhaps the rider reminded her of other deaths. Death of the spirit, of the heart. She lay awake, the bedside light holding night at bay, the clock defying silence, until day released her into sleep.

At ten o'clock she was astonished and greatly reassured to find herself alive and hungry. Had Betty or Janet, her daughters, been there she could have told them. But preoccupied with husbands, children and households they lived miles away. Needing some sensible person to say 'Nonsense!', and mean it, Mrs Mannering made an appointment with Dr Parker for that afternoon.

Watching the needle rise, watching him pump up his little machine which tightened the tight band on her upper arm, she gave a deprecatory laugh.

'I had a nightmare last night,' she said lightly.

'What did you eat for supper?' he asked easily.

'Oh – a small tin of lobster, with a winter salad.'

He shook his head, smiling, admonishing.

'I'm surprised you didn't have ten nightmares', and then gaily, jocularly, to the comeliness she still carried like a banner, 'you may fool the world about your age, Julie, but you'll never fool your digestion. There's no change out of sixty-four for either of us. Did I tell you I was retiring at Easter?'

He scribbled hieroglyphics, and said her blood pressure was all right.

'Really? Truly?' trying to decipher the code, and his expression.

'I'd tell you if it weren't. Look a damn fool if I kidded you and then you went down with high blood pressure, wouldn't I?'

'Yes. Yes, of course.'

'Heart's in better shape than mine. Lungs O.K. Did you give the nurse a sample of water? Good. Look here, Julie. It will take about a week to get an overall picture – results of blood tests, and so on. But I'll eat my forceps if there's anything wrong with you.'

He sat back in his swivel chair and looked at her.

'You're not getting some foolish notion about cancer, are you? Every other woman who comes to me these days seems to think she's got cancer.'

'No, no. No.'

'No giddiness, fainting fits, headaches, pains?'

'None – just a bad dream.'

He chuckled.

'Lobster,' he said, writing out a prescription. 'Take one of these if you can't sleep. They're so mild as to be almost useless. Are you worried about anything else?'

The rider, holding his pale horse between his knees. The long silence in the dark.

'No, Donald,' she said stoutly. 'It must have been the lobster, as you say.

As he showed her out he said, 'If every patient was in your condition I should have retired years ago.'

At the corner of the windy road she met the vicar, and clutched at comfort. For over two years she had been embroidering an altar cloth exquisitely. Was responsible for the flowers in the church. So kept him shivering politely in the autumn air, talking of nothing, wasting his time that was not his own. But he could not, he regretted, walk home with her for tea. His ever-patient wife waited. He had a choir practice very early this evening. Some other time he would be delighted. Delighted.

'I must really finish the altar cloth,' she cried, out of blackmail.

'So *very* kind,' he murmured guiltily, 'so *very* accomplished. We shall think of you every time we look at it.'

Like a memorial.

'Oh I'm not dead yet,' she laughed, too high for amusement.

He was shocked to think that she should have thought he meant ... Good gracious, these days, the three score years and ten was a mockery ...

'Are you not feeling well, Mrs Mannering?' he asked solicitously.

'I slept badly last night,' she said. Quieter, ashamed. 'But apparently I am in the best of health, so Dr Parker tells me. And doctors know, don't they? Nothing escapes them, ever, does it?'

He took her arm and drew her nearer to the wall, out of the bitter wind.

'Now if I may telephone my good wife from your house I will take you up on the offer of tea,' he said.

His time was never his own, but belonged to other people.

'The dream was so clear,' said Mrs Mannering, clattering the cake tin down on the kitchen table, something she would not normally do, who served all meals to tempt and beguile.

'I heard the voice. I felt the touch on my shoulder. I saw the rider. This, surely, is *your* province', she persisted, noticing his wet shoes, his cold red fingers on the warmth of the kitchen cup.

'But what am I doing,' she cried, distracted, 'allowing you to drink from a kitchen cup?'

'It does not matter, Mrs Mannering. We are concerned with more important events than teacups.'

'Dr Parker thought it was the lobster. The result of eating tinned lobster, though I made a winter salad, and thin bread and butter. By myself, of course, upon a tray. I did not have fresh lobster, naturally. All for myself, and such a price. Though perhaps he meant the lobster itself, and not the fact that it was tinned.'

Sitting down suddenly, unmindful of the cake upon the table, the kitchen crockery, 'This was a message for me, and I am afraid.'

'We are all afraid of the unknown,' he said slowly, dropping crumbs, 'but as practising Christians, believing in an afterlife by the side of which this earthly life pales . . .'

'Oh do *not*,' she said, 'use that word, Mr Kenyon. And besides – I am not sure, not absolutely certain of an afterlife. Not when it comes to the final pinch. In church, or when one is young, or does not think too much about it, heaven seems very pleasant. But somehow – faced with the prospect – I am unable to relish it.'

'Perhaps,' he said, looking wistfully into his empty cup, for the wind had been very cold, 'this ... vision ... is merely a reminder to tidy up the odds and ends of problems that beset us. Take it as such. A friendly reminder from the Almighty. Though I am sure you have many useful and happy years before you. Simply, He wishes you to be ready. The bridegroom who awaits the Wise Virgins, if you remember ... the oil in the lamps ...'

'It is four decades,' said Mrs Mannering with a dry air, 'since I was young and virginal. And I have never claimed to be wise.'

'But in His eyes we are all children.'

'Suddenly everything seems to have withdrawn from me.'

She remembered to offer more tea, which was accepted.

'I have lived as good a life as I was able. I have brought up three children, all doing well. My husband had every care and comfort. My house was open to friends and family. I have been, I think you may agree, a devoted member of the Church, though brought up a Methodist which is somewhat different. Still, it is the same God.'

And she must die?

'I had rather have known nothing about it. I had rather have died in my sleep, not knowing. I do not wish to know.'

He was helpless, moistening his forefinger to pick up crumbs.

'Whenever you feel troubles,' he said, 'my wife and I ...'

'The last enemy,' she said sadly.

'Perhaps the last friend?'

She shook her head.

'I should be less than honest if I agreed with you.'

She saw his hand move towards his hat, and then draw away.

'You have been so kind,' she said. 'You have been very kind.'

'I feel so useless, and did so much want to help.'
'You have done your best. No one can do more.'
'And any time, Mrs Mannering. Any time.'
For his time was never his own.

On an impulse she packed a suitcase and spent a week
with her elder daughter. She wanted to be wanted so that
she could be hidden. For in this cramped spare room, with
its sprigged curtains and painted furniture, she felt safe.
The rider could hardly cross a strange threshold, unbidden.
Would not, surely, think to seek her here.

In the noise of everyday family life, full of comforting
detail, she made herself pleasant and useful. And discovered
that they were whole without her. She was welcome to
come, and welcome to go. This was not her life but theirs.

Later she visited her other daughter, and then her son.
And in each house, though wanted for herself, she was not
wanted for them. She came home. Bent her head over the
altar cloth for hours and hours. Finished it.

'Why?' she asked herself, 'why?'

For what was the point of life if it ended? And what was
the use? It had been after all, a very ordinary business. She
had done nothing of importance, after all.

The clock ticked briskly at her hours, the calendar tore
harshly at her days, the seasons turned towards empti-
ness.

She suffered the bitterest sorrow of all, that pity for the
self. Poor self who had dreamed of so much, so freshly, in
the days that were past. Drowned in a sea of washing and
ironing and cooking and mending and cleaning; in homely
loving and domestic chatter. Who at the end was unwanted,
by those in whom it had lost itself. The talents buried. The
promise unfulfilled.

At the end of the month she took her altar cloth to the
vicarage and received their gratitude.

'How are you feeling, Mrs Mannering?' the vicar asked,
eyes troubled.

He had failed her.

'I think,' she said gently, driven back upon herself, 'it must have been the lobster.'

She had not failed *him*.

'We cannot weigh a weight of fire, nor measure a measure of wind,' he ruminated, 'nor call again the day that is past. So how should we be expected to understand? We can but accept it, with courage and cheerfulness, and such charity as we possess.'

'I was overwrought,' said Mrs Mannering. 'I must ask you to forgive me.'

That afternoon she walked into the city's biggest art shop and chose an impressive selection of oil paints. This extravagance, hardly justified, would curtail some necessity. But that was not important. Pointless to buy a new winter coat, if it should be worn only for a season. And lest her ambition, once so overpowering as to burn within her, should have gone to cinders, she bought a book called *How to Paint in Oils*.

Call me again the day that is past. Call me that day. That day when after school hours, in the school theatre, unexpectedly released, she had painted scenery until her hand cramped. That day when seeing a festival of colour take fire upon a canvas she had cried, 'Who is this?' and they told her. *Matthew Smith*. Call me again those days that are past. But not, and this of course was the inevitable gall, not that day when her father taking thought for the future said, 'You shall learn shorthand and typing, and paint in your spare time.' For of course there had never been any spare time. Time was not given but taken, or else flew on to remind you at a later turning that you had done nothing.

She tracked down three old and awful pictures, priced at a few shillings each, and insisted upon carrying them home herself that moment.

'These are lovely pictures, lady,' said the junkshop dealer, rummaging. 'You've got an Eye for Art, you have.'

An Eye for Art? These orange sunsets blazing upon wistful maidens? These stage cows, stumble-footed in improbable pink clover? This Highland Glen so brown and

wracked and gloomy as to strike terror into the heart of the
most fanatical Scot?

'Good heavens,' cried Mrs Mannering, 'I have not
bought them for their Art but for their Frames.'

She also purchased canvas, size and drawing pins. At five
o'clock she had tea in a café, looking out of the window at
passers-by.

She worked through the evening with increasingly nimble
fingers, creating three fine white dazzling stretches of un-
painted space. With regret she ate and bathed and climbed
into bed. The first picture forming in her mind, she prayed
that she might live until the morning.

Donald Parker found her absorbed and rapt, a day's
washing up stacked on the draining board, her fingers bright
with colour. She wiped her hands impatiently upon a rag.

'I've come to ask you how you feel, you disgustingly
healthy woman,' he cried. Fresh, pink and cold from the
frost.

'You can't look until this is finished,' she said first, turning the canvas away from him, and then, 'so you think that
doctors know everything?'

'Do patients know more?'

'Sometimes. But I'm grateful that you should call,
Donald, and thank you again.'

'I didn't know you were an artist.'

'Possibly I am not, but I enjoy painting.'

He was puzzled, who had always been urged to stay and
talk. Absentmindedly she offered coffee, and was thankful
that he refused.

'Evelyn and I have been thinking,' he said, 'you are very
much alone these days. Would you like to have supper with
us, one evening next week?'

'I should love to. On Tuesday and Thursday I am going
to the theatre. Otherwise I am free.'

'Good Lord. Have you come into a legacy, Julie?'

'No,' she replied coolly, 'but I have *cashed* a legacy and
intend to spend it on myself rather than on someone else's
future.'

He sat down unbidden.

'What's wrong with you, Julie?'

She hesitated, but years of confidences, unbroken, lay between them in a friendly chain.

'I dreamed I was going to die, and it seemed very final, and no one could help me. Then it seemed to me that only I could help me, and I thought of the buried talents and dug one of them up. So that I should not go empty-handed, as it were. It is a little rusty, but the pleasure is as great as ever.'

'Julie, there is nothing physically wrong with you.'

'I believe you. But we only know the unimportant things such as prices and weather. The great events happen outside our reckoning. I am quite aware that this house needs redecorating, for instance. And part of me is horrified at what I am doing instead. But inside, where I really know, I feel my way is right. In the end even our absurdity must be our own.'

He shrugged.

'Spare us an evening, anyway. Ring Evelyn and fix it up.'

'Thank you, both. I shall ring her tomorrow.'

He shook his head, knew she waited for him to be gone, and went.

Call me again the day that is past. There were so many to be recalled. Tapers of happiness, illuminating the grey and dark of her remembrance. The feeling of exaltation when she gave birth. The sense of being one impregnable fortress with Jack, in the early years of their marriage. The immense significance of a jug of milk on a kitchen table in the morning sun. Of laughter, and joy that was too deep for laughter. Of sadness so wild and bitter that it purged and left her cleansed. Of faces and friendships and blessed kindness. Of new beginnings after old quarrels.

All these had been felt by legions before her, and would be felt by legions ahead of her. And suddenly, painting stolidly away at the *Still Life* which would never in a thousand years so much as touch the hem of Matthew Smith's shining robe, she sensed the rider on his pale horse.

The room was choked in silence.

But I am living so vividly now, she thought. Why?

Very slowly, keeping tight hold of her palette and brush for courage, she faced him. And he inclined his helm, obdurate but courtly. They knew each other, he and she. The mail glove rested lightly on the bridle of the horse. And the horse itself was fell and beautiful beyond belief. The dark soft eyes. The creamy coat. The trappings very fine and fair. Oh, how she would love to paint ... but not in a million years ... not even Matthew Smith ... perhaps Rembrandt ... never she. Between the vision and the canvas blundered her inarticulate brush. There he stood, an integral part of the life he would end. Was he the last mystery? Or merely the messenger? The signpost which pointed elsewhere.

The tapers blowing in the night wind. The uncharted seas.

She recalled her jewelled days and their brilliance was heightened. It seemed to her now, sharpened by eternity, that never had any woman been so blessed. How could she not have known? So busy in experience that the reckoning was never taken. Such a life, she thought with pride, worthy to be reaped even by the fourth horseman of the Apocalypse.

'When and as you please, then,' said Mrs Mannering, and sat upon a chair in order to die as seemly as possible.

Was there a glimmer of humour beneath the helm? Or had he conveyed the message intended? That she should, in face of death, make the most of that time left to her. That she should in nowise regret a life as plain and good as bread and butter. Both were needful.

Horse and rider wheeled. She watched them become infinitely small, and though she was relieved she felt regretful. As one who has entertained royalty expectedly to tea remembers that nothing went wrong. As one who has entertained royalty expectedly to tea, on a suburban estate, finds the house smaller when they have gone.

The vicar, driven by his own nature and the nature of his calling, found her contemplating a very pleasing little painting of a bowl of fruit, two empty wine bottles, and an evening paper.

'What talent!' he cried, delighted to praise.

She, turning with new eyes, found even his harrassment precious to the sight.

'You seem happier,' he said, relieved by one person at least who was not bent on asking of him.

'I have discovered,' said Mrs Mannering demurely, 'that I can call again the day that is past.'

His humour and wisdom tickled, the vicar said, 'And is that profitable?'

'I have found,' said Mrs Mannering, contemplating with enjoyment the second canvas, 'that it heightens the day that is present, and casts light upon the day which is to come.'

Seeing her bringing forth the best cups in his honour he said, as dryly and demurely as she had answered him, 'Then all that is needful is to weigh fire and measure the wind, and you will have your answer.'

'Ah! Coffee walnut cake. My favourite,' momentarily distracted.

'Perhaps,' he continued gently, 'you might enlighten *me*, who am often in the dark.'

And settled down to partake of less exalted fare.

Biographical Notes

Brian Glanville

born in London, 1931, and educated at Charterhouse. He lived in Italy from 1952–55 and regularly goes back there. Now married, with four young children, he lives in Holland Park. He wrote his first novel, *The Reluctant Dictator*, at 18; it was published in 1952. *Henry Sows the Wind* was next, followed by the first to get serious attention, *Along the Arno*, about expatriates in Florence. *A Cry of Crickets* (1970) is in some senses a sequel, though the characters are quite different. Other novels: *The Bankrupts* and *Diamond* have Anglo-Jewish themes. *A Second Home*, about an actress, and *A Roman Marriage* are both narrated in the first person by women. *After Rome, Africa*, an entertainment, set in Calabria, was published in 1959, *The Artist Type* in 1967, *The Rise of Gerry Logan*, a novel about a soccer player, in 1963, *The Olympian*, its protagonist a runner, in 1969. The Americans saw the allegorical point, the English didn't.

He has published three collections of short stories: *A Bad Streak* in 1961, which included the first serious fiction about professional football to be published in Britain, *The Director's Wife*, 1963, and *The King of Hackney Marshes*, 1965.

He has been writing about sport for the *Sunday Times* since 1958, covering four World Cups and three Olympiads; the last in Mexico City, 1968 where the grotesque juxtaposition with the student massacre made him promise to go to no more.

Janice Elliott

born in a Derbyshire village in 1931 and brought up in Nottingham. She read English at St Anne's College, Oxford, and worked as a journalist for eight years on various magazines, and on the *Sunday Times*, which she left to devote herself to writing. She has published eight novels, *The Godmother* *The Somnambulists*, *Cave with Echoes*, *The Buttercup Chain* (filmed in 1970), *The Singing Head*, *Angels Falling*, *The Kindling*, *A State of Peace* and a children's book *The Birthday Unicorn*. She is also a critic and broadcaster, reviews fiction for the *Sunday Telegraph*, contributes stories and articles to many newspapers and magazines and writes a regular personal column for *Twentieth Century*. She is married, has one son, and lives in a sixteenth-century cottage in Sussex.

Jennifer Dawson

born in 1929 and brought up chiefly in South London. She read History at Oxford, Philosophy at London University, and has been a social worker in a mental hospital, taught in schools in England and France, has been an indexer, a hospital cleaner and a sub-editor on a children's encyclopaedia. Her first novel *The Ha Ha* was published in 1961 and won the James Tait Black Memorial prize and she has published two other novels, *Fowler's Snare* (1962) and *The Cold Country* (1965). She is married, lives in Oxford and is currently writing a new novel *Strawberries and Slum Clearance*.

Paul Winstanley

born in 1936. He has worked in a variety of fields including scrap metal, motorcycle mechanics, demolition and journalism, the last including the features-editorships of *Town*, *Woman's Mirror* and the *Weekend Telegraph*. He was in the navy, read Philosophy and English at Newcastle, and is now a carpenter. His fiction has been published in *Town* and *Nova*.

Jean Stubbs

born in Lancashire, the daughter of a University lecturer, and educated at Manchester High School and Manchester College of Art. She has two children, lives in Wimbledon, and claims to have written her first novel, *The Rose Grower*, on the tube train on the way to work. This was followed by *The Travellers* and *Hanrahan's Colony*, both about the peripheral society that haunts old up-and-down houses. After this, she wrote *The Straw Crown*, about the exposure of a naïve island society to the intolerable pressures of twentieth-century publicity, *The Grand Enemy* based on the life of the eighteenth-century paricide Mary Blandy, and *The Passing Star*, a novel on the life of Eleonora Duse. Her last book was *The Case of Kitty Ogilvie*, a fictional reconstruction of an historic tragedy. She is just completing a book on the early life of Henry VII, to be entitled *An Unknown Welshman*.

More About Penguins

Penguinews, which appears every month, contains details of all the new books issued by Penguins as they are published. From time to time it is supplemented by *Penguins in Print*, which is a complete list of all available books published by Penguins. (There are well over three thousand of these.)

A specimen copy of *Penguinews* will be sent to you free on request, and you can become a subscriber for the price of the postage. For a year's issues (including the complete lists) please send 30p if you live in the United Kingdom, or 60p if you live elsewhere. Just write to Dept EP, Penguin Books Ltd, Harmondsworth, Middlesex, enclosing a cheque or postal order, and your name will be added to the mailing list.

Note: *Penguinews* and *Penguins in Print* are not available in the U.S.A. or Canada

Penguin Modern Stories

1. William Sansom   Jean Rhys   David Plante   Bernard Malamud
2. John Updike   Sylvia Plath   Emanuel Litvinoff
3. Philip Roth   Margaret Drabble   Jay Neugeboren Giles Gordon
4. Sean O'Faolain   Nadine Gordimer   Shiva Naipaul Isaac Babel
5. Penelope Gilliat   Benedict Kiely   Andrew Travers Anthony Burton
6. Elizabeth Taylor   Dan Jacobson   Maggie Ross   Robert Nye
7. Anthony Burgess   Susan Hill   Yehuda Amichai B. S. Johnson
8. William Driver   A. L. Barker   C. J. Driver
9. V. S. Pritchett   Ruth Fainlight   Frederick Busch Mel Calman

Not for Sale in the U.S.A. or Canada